THIRTEEN MONTHS

Jane De Croos

Edited by Dr Charles Clarke

Cover by Pearl De Croos

COPYRIGHT © 2019
JANE DE CROOS

All rights reserved.

ISBN:

DEDICATION

For Pearl & Boh

ACKNOWLEDGMENTS

To my daughter Pearl for all the nights in bed together with you working on the front cover and your continuous enthusiasm. For these moments we shared I will always treasure. To Jola for his insightful poem, thank you for sharing your wisdom. And not forgetting, Seamus Ruttledge all the way out in Tuam, Co. Galway for the song lyrics I can still hear you sing. To Giuliano Sacchi, London's finest acupuncture to whom I went to when I wanted to start writing, without you this never would have happened. To Dr Charles Clarke who was very kind and thorough on the edit. And of course to all my lovely friends who did the numerous read-throughs and told me where I was going wrong. (If you have any complaints about the book...please see them).

And lastly, to my twin sister Jilly...for this is our story, a story that I've loved every minute of.

1 JANUARY

"If April be the cruelest month."

> The Wasteland, T.S. Eliot.

January is by far the darkest.

Crystal watches a cigarette burn down in a filthy old plastic Heineken ashtray. It's a Marlborough Silver, for a non-smoker she's particular. She opens the black tin that that sits proudly on the National TV and takes out a little white plastic ball. Her heart thumps steadily; her stomach does a little squelch. She looks across at Bally in the threadbare armchair, she's leaning forward over an empty plastic water bottle on the table, pin-pricking the foil she's placed over the neck. Bally's her best friend, her only friend.

"Well that's us done for another year mate," Bally's voice is proper posh. Crystal has never gotten used to it. They've stuck it out in the pub for nearly two hours drinking overpriced, bad quality vodka, in dishwasher warm glasses. It hadn't been busy, The Black Ram, was never busy, it was just short of glasses, always had been.

"Itz not 'ver yeahh... still got a 'hole fuckin 'our to go," Cyrstal flicked her wrist over. Her timepiece was big, heavy and looked expensive. She was drunk, they both were.

"My deeeearest Crystal how eloquently put."

"Yah yah yah! Bally woz your New Yeeears resolution? To be more of a cunt than you already 're? 'Ow 'bout clean your flat? Oh no you can't cause this ain't a flat, wot isit Bally, where are we?" Crystal laughs out loud at her own joke, whilst pretending to tickle her ribs. Bally's finger salute is swift and to the point.

"I'm gonna be more of a cunt than normal, that's easier."

"Haha easier than findin' a word for what we're sittin' in!" The jokiness between them is slightly strained; they both know it and it's got nothing to do with what was just said.

"I'm gonna get"...Bally's voice trails off. Everything forgotten, they're both distracted, their minds far, far away in another place. They want to go to that place together.

Scooping fag ash very gently into a well in the foil, she nods at Crystal who passes the open wrap along the stained glass coffee table. Bally opens the wrap and sighs, her breath quickens and she feels the joy building. On goes a good size rock and after exhaling slowly she places her mouth over one of the openings she made in the side of the bottle and flicks the lighter.

Inhale...the smoke plumes into the bottle arhhhh, into her mouth, into her lungs into her blood stream, into her brain. The hit is marvellous... ahhhhhh! How can that plasticy taste be so good? And it's so very good! Thumb over the mouth hole and exhale, her lung capacity is spectacular. Crystal has her own bottle sorted and now it's her turn. Ahhh so good, a smile creeps over her face. Her head thumps back on the sofa. And they start laughing and smiling and loving life, the earlier tension between them fading with each plumed exhalation.

Sip, sip out of Evian bottles. Laugh, laugh chat, chat!

Their pipes smoking...ahhhhh, it all looks so pretty! One hit, two hit three hits, four. Then more, lots more, the travel clock by the mattress across the room on the floor ticks tocks. Time passes as Lou Reed chats about Jane and Jimmy and alleyways.

Bally's flat is tiny and grotty, damp patches stain the walls in the bedroom/living room and the shower trickles a coldish stream, perfect on those 3 hot summer nights a year. There are no lights in the kitchen and as you walk around the flat the £6 red Argos lamp flickers on and off in the hallway. If you need to see anything in the kitchen when the sun isn't shinning, you have to angle the lamp into the galley space. The kitchen and the toilet have the only windows. The kitchen sash is quite big and looks out onto the stairwell, it's where everyone on the other side of the building smokes whatever they're smoking. Their voices amplified in the small narrow well. The separate toilet has a tiny sash window which was painted half open a long time ago. You can just about fit both your hands through it and touch the red brick wall opposite, that's always warm.

The bathroom is bright white and sterile. The tiles are white the towels are white; there are two of them.

The main room has a mattress on the floor in one corner with a dresser and wardrobe pushed up next to each other. There's a sofa opposite in an alcove bit with an armchair for when people come over. This divides the room sleeping one end, entertaining the other. There's a very low coffee table in front of the sofa. Everything is very low, one lamp by the TV that can swivel so you can watch in bed or on the sofa and one lamp by the bed.

Nearly Thirteen Months

Ballys eyes suddenly lit up,"What d'ya think about what Tony said tonight, about his new bird wanting him to do the ole rape fantasy, well apart from the obvious?"

"I'm with ya Bally babe 'hoo, or should I say wot, would wanna do that in der first place?" This gets the girls giggling and making loud retching sounds. Bally leans forward, rock in hand and Crystal knows it's theory time. She's never met anyone who theorises or smokes so much. The two are definitely positively correlated. "Don't tell me you gotta theory 'bout 'rape fantasy', shut the fuck up mate?" She says to her mate.

"Funnily enough I do and it goes like this: Girl finds boy's bedroom performance a bit lack lustre. Specifically in the 'fuck me, nail me to the mattress, make it hurt' department. She can't say to him directly that his routine is more Romeo than rodeo keeping in mind Romeo never even got a finger in. And that she's in danger of falling asleep and possibly never waking up for a 100 years, because he's so fucking dull, keeping in mind, it was the tiniest of pricks that got Snow White into that shit. So she can't tell him directly cause of the 'fragile male ego' thing and she knows if she were to tell him he'd a) call her a frigid dike, b) get in a mood and pull out the silent treatment c) unravel irrevocably." Bally's speech is fast paced and furious, her face serious and questioning, the delivery is superb and Crystal looks like she's going to pee herself.

"So she tells him, whispers in his pathetic little ear, how she'd like to be raped. How she'd like him to come up behind her in the flat, whilst she's washing up, grab her by her ponytail, yank her head back, wrap a pair of tights quickly round her head, between her teeth, forcing her mouth wide open, tying them tightly. Within seconds they're causing the sides of her mouth to bleed. She's getting wet. He's panting hard, she's too shocked to move, waiting for his next move. He spins her round and BANG goes his hand across her face, crashing against her ear whipping her cheek, fuck that hurts and it's so horny.

BANG he backhands slapping her again on her other cheek, her head whips back face stinging. She's dizzy and exhausted, weak on her feet he hauls her the few steps to the kitchen table and pushes her face down across the cheap scratched pine, her nose is bleeding, she's choking on her own blood and spit. He slows down, breathing hard, one hand on her back, the other pulling at her jeans and pants dragging them down, tugging them off one leg at a time. She's naked from the waist down. Then he fucks her," Bally pauses breathing heavily, her mouth slightly open.

"And?"

"But by this point the victims got bored of his

sexual advances, leans over for the remote control in their open plan living room and switches on the TV. The moment has evaded them...'*Yay! Corries on...What the fuck..what's her face is getting well pissed again.*"

The girls go into spasms of laughter, the crying snot type. Bally wipes her eyes and nose on her armchair cover.

"Bally your a fuckin twat. I woz well gettin' off on 'at one...brilliant," Crystal giggles, recovering slightly. And they laugh and they joke and they smoke out of their little homemade bottles. Time passes and neither notice and neither care.

Many hours later...

"What goes up must come down," Bally sing songs. She picks up one of the foil sheets and wraps it around the chopstick that lives on the table, which is there especially for the purpose of making a thin foil tube. She pulls out an olive sized ball from the black tin, she likes the size, this ones in blue plastic. How thoughtful she thinks to colour code. Gently, gently prise it open, tap, tap -- the gear hits the foil, tish, tish. Heat, tilt, inhale, let it run, it must always be running, follow the plume, it's all about the inhalation, chase it, it must never get away...and relax... ahhhh that's so good. Hmmmm lets have some more.

"Time for beddy bye byes, Bally dancer," Crystal whispers to her friend smiling. The clock tick tocks, Bally lifts her hand and slurs something.

New Years day dawns late without Bally who comes round in the afternoon after managing to get to her bed sometime earlier. She always manages to get to bed. She never looks at the clock unless she's working. Bally has a crap job that everyone thinks is good. She works solely on her own and defends the lowest of the low, she barely scrapes a living. She takes the cases that her Clerks' put her way, they know she's bright and can work the cases in her sleep (if they only knew, she practically did). Her lifestyle never comes into question as dark circles under her eyes and transparent, greasy skin are what young criminal barristers, working hard cases, look like.

Bally's 31, with beautiful long reddish brown thick hair. But whilst being nearly translucent on the outside, with her pale white bluish skin with not a blemish on it, she's a thick layer of clouded shite on the inside. She knows this. Leaning against the kitchen wall heating up a Tesco Finest iced coffee in the microwave a slight wave of guilt wafts over her starting near her stomach, gently sweeping over her heart, heading for her brain.

"No, no, no you fucking don't, not today," her voice is croaky and hoarse, sometimes she doesn't speak for days.

"Bye, bye conscience I've got work to do." Back in bed, under the covers, she flips open a blue file next to her bed, sloshing coffee on to the first page, wiping it with her sleeve she reads 'Jonathan Price Defendant'.

"Fuckin hell not him again," she sighs slowly. Jonathon Price was a nasty little thug; she was probably going lose this one. She sometimes lost her cases, this wasn't the movies.

Night time draws in, wrapping the little flat in a protective cover as Bally mentally flicks into another gear. She speed reads, rapidly turning pages, willing an angle to jump out. There might be some little thing; she knows she always gives it her best shot. She's proud of herself and gets out of bed for a little treat, a little shot perhaps? The Vladivar lives in the freezer, there are a few 350ml bottles packed into the little ice shelf above the fridge, that's never had anything in it. There are four Nutella glass jars in the cupboard. Using one of these she pours the cold syrup till the glass is half full. Sip, sip, gulp, gulp, it feels good. She tops up and then shuffles back to bed. Bally does everything in bed. Only when Crystal comes round does she sit in her armchair. She smirks, thinking of her buddy. Last night was good fun, they'd missed the New Years Eve bit, but who gives a shit.

She's always admired Crystal, remembers when they first met at The Black Ram, her local in Soho.

Crystal was 34, it was two years ago. She looked good, well turned out and in control, she was on her own and drawing an audience. They got talking, they got drinking, they went and scored. Crystal had some dollar and Bally had the chitty chat and that was that. Crystal had told her in a matter of fact way, on that first night in Bally's flat, about her childhood.

Her mother had been on the game, drank heavily and neglected her daughter. Crystal had often looked after her mother and started earning money from various enterprises when she very young. They had lived together in an over-furnished two bed council flat in the Angel. Crystal was sixteen when she moved out into her own apartment. She still saw her mum regularly, always gave her a few quid. Bally was blown away by the nonjudgemental attitude towards her mum as Crystal said, "She did her best under the circumstances." Crystal was from proper working-class stock and proud of it and Bally was awed by her incredible drive, her conviction and her acceptance of her lot. But, what she liked about her most of all, was she was quite easily the smartest human being she had ever met. Hence, the nickname Crystal, her real name was Caroline, but everyone called her Crystal, because she was a cut above the rest.

Crystal was a genius at making money, running a business as a staff training motivational coach.

Nearly Thirteen Months

She worked for the big city firms, charged a fortune and made a positive difference to bank balances, theirs and hers. She'd written a book on motivation, which had been in the top 10 Sunday Times list for ever and she was in major demand for TV interviews and the like. Crystal was a modern day female entrepreneur and the darkest horse Bally had ever come across.

The vodka warms and energises. She looks for the buzz, which is fast on an empty stomach. It's Friday, day off tomorrow. Yay no work...treat time she thinks to herself.

Up again for the black box, the sight of cigarette ash piled on a little plate makes her truly happy. Back to bed, she leans over to the CD player and slips in Shaved Fish, whir, whir goes the machine. Sip, sip, flick, flick...She's on the run. The clock by the bed tick tocks.

Some time later...

General Levi's shouting 'Incredible' and hiccupping loudly, she looks at her phone in a daze. He's at the door. For someone who's spent the last twenty hours lying down, she gets up a bit too sudden, crashes across the flat, narrowly misses head butting the wall and buzzes him in. He's drunk, 'that's handy', she thinks, as he stumbles on the first steps up, as he won't notice her being slightly tipsy. Not that he'd notice anyway, selfish, self-absorbed cunt. She sees her very own theatre production at the Royal Palladium unfold.

Act 1, Scene 1:

Mr Daniel Wright staggers up the apartment narrow stairs holding onto frail banister with bottle of vodka in hand. He trips up the last steps, falls forward crushing his head against the doorframe, killing himself instantly. The vodka bottle drops to the carpeted floor and rolls into the flat intact.

"Alright Dan?" she whispers, he doesn't hear her and his voice is loud and offensive next to hers.

"Bally Girl, where's my little dancer? I wanna fuck, nice an slooooowwww."

As he said that last bit drool hung from his mouth. He was disgusting, he was turning her on, she stepped back and beckoned him in with a narrow finger.

"Come to me Danny, you know what I want," she leaned back using the wall as suppor, standing up unaided was not really working for her, right now! He was on her quick, hands everywhere, she did nothing barely responded. He had no problem picking up her slight frame and dropping to his knees on the, mattress. He shed his shoes, trousers, pants like a sheaf, his shirt took longer, quite a lot longer, he couldn't find the buttons, that's what happens when you're very drunk. She didn't help him and waited for him to undress her, her tracksuit bottoms and thin top were off in seconds she wasn't wearing underwear and as she didn't have any buttons to find. Thank Christ for that she thought. She didn't know if she could witness anymore button search.

Bally always felt weird until they were both naked in bed between the crisp white sheets in the room with no window. The duvet is bright white and fluffy. He got inside her by spitting on his hand. Over his shoulder she had a good view of the ceiling and could see a dragon's head in the mould with smoke pouring out its mouth. It's a Chinese dragon, well she is in Soho. The heavy breathing starts, panting on top of her like a pig that's what he's doing, it disgusting, he's disgusting. But Bally is used to being disgusted, as he's panting on top of her she imagines him as a big, filthy, scratchy pig with a dribbling snout, it's the only way she can get off. Now she loses herself in his disgustingness. The fat, disgusting, sweating pig. She's never understood why it turns her on. She opens her legs wider as wide as she can get them, feet firmly on the mattress and for the first time lifts her hips to slam into him. Arghh it turns her on, arghhh he's a fucking disgusting pig, ugghhh he groans, he loves it when she comes, it makes him feel like a real man. Ballys fucking gorgeous.

End of Act:

The gentlemen withdraws impolitely and then fucks off. Bally wipes her sticky crutch on the crumpled bed sheets and falls into a deep sleep.

Tuesday morning comes in slowly creeping up the side of the flat, greeting the damp on its way. Good morning it says looking down upon the tangled mess on the bed. Bally waves an ineffectual greeting using two fingers at the damp and after a quick shower under the trickle and a lukewarm microwave coffee she hauls the heavy file into her already full wheelie bag and knocks it down the narrow staircase. It's always so heavy; she can feel it dragging on her soul. The January fresh air isn't cold or biting, it's a mild nondescript day with a nondescript car accident involving a nondescript drunk driver. Everything is the same. On the pavement she strides purposefully to the tube. Her Chambers are in Chancery Lane, so she takes the Central Line, the red one, the period line. Blob, blob, blob. She hasn't had her period for ages and wonders what happened to it.

Down the road, her black low heels tap. She wears cheap tights, cheap skirt, cheap blouse and a beautiful knee length, navy blue cashmere coat, with an enormous fur lined collar, wrapped tightly round her thin frame. With her hair scrapped back into a long thick russet pony tail, she looks gaunt, but her cheeks brighten in the air and her blue eyes nearly sparkle. She's got that Irish skinned milk completion that makes her look a bit see through, but today she's ok.

Dragging her wheelie up the steps to Chambers, she greets her colleagues after the too short Christmas break. Number 46 is a medium sized Chambers that does all sorts, Johnny a chirpy looking clerk catches her in the hallway…"pigeon hole" he shouts, walking briskly past her. The place buzzes. It's positively throbbing. She's in court at 10am round the corner, just in time to grab a coffee. She can feel herself waking up, the buzz is infectious.

All on time, meet the client, shake hands, she knows hers are clammy but she's feeling good. She defends to the best of her ability, but it's not enough. Her client is found guilty, she doesn't really care. The sickness comes on quick, arghh her stomach knots nearly doubling her over, argghhh she can feel the sweat leaving her skin, soaking her blouse, between her legs, in her tights. Shallow breaths come, inhale slowly focus, calm down. Bolting to the toilet she picks the last cubicle, she always goes in the last cubicle she wretches as quietly as she can over the toilet. The cold tiles soothe as she presses her head against them. She licks them, licks the tiles, big fat licks and inhales slowly. They're wet, her face is wet, spit dribbles down her chin. It turns her on.

Trying to slow her breathing, mmmm her hands slide up and down pushing against her hips, hard nipples, dark pink tingling nipples. Exhaling she counts down from ten slowly rubbing her crutch.... Ahhh she gasps out, ahhhh...she slows, stops, stretches her fingers out, then holds her crutch tight for a few seconds relishing in the pulsing that her grip is creating. Steadying herself against the door she pulls her clothes back into place, her mind is clear and focused as she splashes water on her face. Grrrrrr go get em tiger, she laughs at her reflection and walks out, banging the door behind her. She shakes hands briefly with her clients family and looks sympathetic, then it's back to Chambers for the next assignment she hoped was coming her way.

There was no job waiting for her. Money was already tight, she was practically starving. If it hadn't been for the ridiculously low rent she paid she couldn't live in London or anywhere, come to think of it. Her flat (if you could call it that) was no des res, but it was a pretty cool place to live. Time to go home but first she had to bump into Pete, stock was low and low stock meant anxiety. Anxiety meant reality and no one wanted that, did they? Lou Reed's rough demo track Oh Gin piped up from her pocket, signaling her mother's intent to communicate.

Her Mum (Irene) and Dad (John) lived in the crappy suburbs of Reading, where mini roundabouts and dog shit had been part of her upbringing. Mums side of the family was Irish, all from County Cork and saying they weren't really in touch after her teenage Mammy was pregnant outside wedlock to a local boy was an understatement. Irene came to London pregnant, miscarried and met Bally's Dad all in the space of one week. John was born and bred in Reading. They had her, Bally, ten years later. She was their only child. She noticed herself sighing as she took the call.

"Hi Mum, hows it with you."

"Oh well you know I can't complain." Give it 5 minutes, you won't be able to resist Bally thought. Her mother's thick Cork accent had bizarrely never faded, she was sure she put it on.

"I've had you're Father beneath me feet all day, oh Bally my girl, he tires me out, he does, you know," (edit the above 5mins to 2.4 seconds).

Her parents were both retired school teachers, her mother sighed constantly and her Father stayed out the way. It was a marriage made in heaven, Catholic heaven, both were miserable and both stuck it out.

Bally mentally removed herself and went into automatic, it was the only way she could survive a conversation with the woman who gave birth to her. Bally often wondered why her parents had wanted her so much, when they barely involved themselves in her life at all. She had never known her parents to share a bed, her dad slept in the single room in their three bed semi ever since she could remember. He always acted like he wanted to be somewhere else. He was polite enough and they'd always had a bit of a laugh. But why, why was he so under the thumb at home, it was an ongoing mystery and one she'd given up analysing a long time ago, helped along by her alcohol consumption and drug taking.

Urghhh she was still talking. "Well Bally love, you know we want to see you, so you pop down whenever. Just call before you do cause we never know where we'll be, what with one thing going on and the other."

"Yes Mum…"

"Well we're not just hanging around, waiting for you, to grace us with your presence," Her mother cut in. Her tone had changed.

"I know that…," Her mother cut her off again. Bally knew where this was going, it always went the same way, she took the phone from her ear and looked at the LCD sadly, the word Mum stared back at her. Mum, what did that mean any more. What did that ever mean? She could hear her mother's voice somewhere in the background.

"Well, you were always a selfish one weren't you girl, did as you pleased ever since you were a little girl. Oh yes, I know your type, had your card marked long ago missy, just like your Aunt Mary, yes you two are cut from the same cloth, so you are. Well you've upset me now and what with your father and yourself it's no wonder I suffer with me headaches. I'll be going now; I can't be chatting to you the best part of the day. I might be retired, but there's still a lot to do, not that you'd understand that. Good bye Bally, don't forget I love you and so does your father, even though he can't show it, but he does you know."

"Bye mum," she replied weakly as she heard the line click. She felt totally drained, why did any contact with her mum always turn into that? It's as if her mum hated her, but why, what had she done? She felt close to tears and felt silly and confused for being so emotional. She breathed hard in the mild air, it was so mild for January and she needed it to be biting cold, she needed to feel the cold air sting her face and chill her to her core. Her throat felt parched, her coat was suddenly very heavy. Deep breaths, calm down, deep breaths... go see Pete.

She pushed open the heavy door to the steamy little café restaurant in Fitzrovia, one of the old ones that an Italian family still ran. They used the meeting place often, it was private, everyone knew everyone else. No surprises Pete didn't like surprises. Pete who was the most punctual dealer in town, sat at a little formica red table and stood up to greet her. "'ello girl, you look lovely as always" Pete said the same thing every time they met, however she looked. Pete was a deeply attractive 43 year old man, whom she was deeply attracted to. At 5ft 11 with a shaved head and strong but wiry body, he could have been any man in the street; it was his job to blend in. His smart casual dress code never drew any attention, nor did his mannerism. Calm and polite he was always ready for a laugh and refreshingly to the point. Bally liked him a lot, she wanted him to like her a lot. She sometimes thought he did, then he'd get all distant. He was the dealer after all. They chatted, drank coffee and exchanged mediocre stories as he passed her the drugs in a little gift bag. Crystal would sort the money out separately. Life was good. It would be better if Perfect Pete would take the bait, but hey, who's complaining. She walked down through Soho with a sexy stalk, drugs in pocket, yep life was good.

Pete smiled wryly about his encounter with Bally. What was it about that girl that really flicked his switch, yes she was good looking, but nothing that hot. She was also a hopeless junkie who was destined for trouble. But wow the girl was razor sharp, she had an intellect and a way of seeing the world that made Pete want to hang around her, she was also that little bit vulnerable and didn't even know it. Yeah that was definitely a turn on. Bally was his little love interest. Blimey he chuckled to himself, calm it down mate, you'll be bloody proposing at this rate. Picking up the pace he focused on the day ahead and did his best to forget about Miss Very Sexy Bally.

January tripped by, it got colder. Always go see Pete, Saint Peter, Peter the Rock. And the two met over and over again. And Saint Peter always kept his distance, he was a professional and he didn't get involved with clients, especially ones that made him feel like Bally did. But it was becoming more and more difficult, as she was becoming more and more insistent, oh how he wanted to touch her back as her hand lingered on his arm, stroked his thigh. He couldn't remember the last time a girl had made him so hot under the collar. And the more she came on too him the more he pulled away. What was it about her? That night he dreamt about her mouth.

2 FEBRUARY

"I have nothing to offer anybody except my own confusion."

Jack Kerouac

The girls walked fast, it was freezing, a bitter harsh freezing. They were heading to a little Chinese dive for dinner. Scarves pulled tight, hats on, heads down; they marched through the back streets of Soho. It was so cold Bally couldn't think. She needed to feed, she couldn't remember when she had last eaten a meal, it had been days. And everyone knows, girl cannot live on BBQ Hula Hoops alone. The Crispy uck on Lyle Street, the D had fallen off circa 1980, was a regular haunt for cheapskate locals who enjoyed rubbish service and top notch BBQ pork and rice, anything else and you were taking your life into your own hands. The squid looked like it had been in the window for some time, all 3 of them were substantially lighter on the right-hand side.

Nearly Thirteen Months

The girls banged their way through the door, the windows were steamed up and dripping condensation, the frames were rotting. Bally always thought the old curved panes were beautiful. They looked like something out of a fairy tale. The Elves and The Shoemaker wouldn't have looked out of place here. She made a mental note to look out for an elf sighting and smirked. Crystal caught her and rolled her eyes, Bally lived in her own world, it was pointless even asking her what she found so funny as she already new the answer would be bizarre and since they hadn't topped up, due to the desire to digest, she wisely held her tongue.

They didn't order as they always had the same thing 2 x green tea, 2 x BBQ pork and rice. They wedged themselves into a corner and pulled of a few items, the green teas were already on the table.

"Nobo could learn a lot from this lot," Crystal offered.

"Oh yeah, what like how nobody wants to listen to a moronic waiter," Bally teased.

"Yeah, that'z exactly it mate, why 'm I payin that much doll'r an' still havin' to explain myself, to a dipstick 'ho insists on repeatin' everythin' I say in som' 'igh duh duh duh, borderline hysterical lilt... did I mention pseudo 'God damn mother fuckin'

US of frickin A accent," Crystal's US of frickin A accent was very good.

"No you didn't, but you just have, so I'm clear on that one as well."

"'ere could be a button on the table," Crystal went on enthusiastically "when you've had enough you can press and the waiters head gets blown off, it would be like the X factor, but with a Hammer House of Horror twist." Haha that had them both laughing until their waitress banged down two plates, causing them both to jump and start giggling. It was a feat of exceptional crockery design, how those plates never broke. You might have thought the waitress had overheard their conversation and was pissed off. But all the staff behaved this way, the girls didn't look up and they didn't say thank you. The food was fantastic, it always was, but as soon as it hit Ballys stomach, she felt sick. Take it slowly she thought to herself, she needed to keep this down, if they were gonna get busy tonight. Looking over at Crystal, she had nothing but admiration for her friend who was rapidly clearing her plate, the woman was a machine. On the other side of the table Crystal noticed Bally delicately chop-sticking her dinner down, literally grain by grain, which reminded her of the 10mg Diazapam she had taken an hour before. Just a little something to give you a nice little appetite and take the edge off 'the waiting game'...wonderful!

Plates cleared (finally) sipping tea (fresh pots), the girls waited. It was 8.30pm, the brown 1950s wall clock told them so. And it was far too late to be out on a Friday night in central London. Pete had requested the time and he was a fastidious time keeper. A highly unusual character trait in a drug dealer, as I'm sure you'd agree and to further his amazingness, he was a dealer who had excellent knowledge of the Weights and Measure Act, 1985. The man was worth his weight in gold, and in very high demand. He chose his clients with care, one fuck up and you were off the books. A fuck up could be quite simply phoning when you shouldn't.

Pete worked on an excellent customer relationship basis. He knew what his customers wanted and supplied them in advance (no you did not call him slightly over refreshed at pub closing). He was the professional end users' dealer of choice and London town was filled to the brim with extremely wealthy professional users. Bally and Crystal had got lucky, Pete dealt with much bigger clients and usually would never have bothered with supplying and personally delivering such small amounts, but he did for them. Or should I say he did it for Bally. He was hooked and he didn't even know it.

If the French and Italians were connoisseurs of food and wine the English were the highest authorities on drug taking. In any one evening it was possible to witness exquisitely rolled spliffs, a little aperitif to whet the appetite no doubt. Ecstasy, only the very finest of course would be popped, two at a time whilst being washed down with the beverage of your choice. MDMA crystal would be left in wraps on the table, where socialising and good fun were guaranteed. Cocaine beautifully lined up on dark plates, passed round, groups had their own notes rolled in anticipation.

Bags full of pretty coloured pharmaceuticals.

Perfectly excellent quality crack cocaine.

Heroin, simple and clean...no need to say any more.

Puff puff, snort snort, pop pop and inhale and wait for it....exhale very very very slowly. The sounds of London and no doubt the suburbs and the countryside too. So many members, in this not so exclusive club.

Crystal looked up at Bally and shook her head; the girl really did have trouble staying in the present.

Act 2, Scene 3 (Bally's mind had taken her somewhere far more exciting.)

Pete walks in, looking pretty sexy, (drug dealers are by default sexy to end users.) They're like the Milk Tray Man to the 80's housewife. Your husband is shit in bed, so whilst you're jacked up on Mandies you can fantasize, without guilt about having a man dressed all in black break into your house (fuck the boat bit, too complicated) and fuck you whilst you're half-asleep (no guilt there because you're not even awake). She's feeling horny at the sight of him.

Oops…back to the plot – Pete swaggers in and immediately catches her eye. He walks up to the table and stops to the side of her chair, she turns slightly to the right his crutch is at eye height and she can see his thick cock, through the thin material of his trousers (artistic licence bit, yeah yeah, we all know its freezing out). He unzips and using one hand to hold his top up pulls it out. Its an angry cock, she's seen this type before. Thick veins on the shaft, bulbous purple head and the rims covered in pearly little white spots. It fuckin reeks, sweaty, musky a strongly filthy odour, its late, the shower he had was this morning, she knows she's gonna taste the piss on it. She licks her lips.

Ooops who's talking to her…

"Bally, Oi Bally…wake up girl, come on girl I need you with me for this one," Pete's working class, slightly put on, inner city London accent comes across the airwaves.

Bally stands up as Pete leans into her, slipping his hand in her pocket. Kiss, kiss, she lingers her kiss, which is enough to get Pete pulling back fast, this all causes Crystal sighs audibly. Bally was always so fuckin desperate for cock. Pete was the dealer, they all knew the rules. You never fuck your dealer...never! Crystal always paid for the drugs in advance but never did the deal, whoever might be watching would struggle to see what went on. Safety first.

Within moments they're heading towards the door, arms flying into coats, scarves being pulled tight. Pete's already left. Crystal leaves £20 on the table which the waitress scoops up grunting. Bally wonders whether she makes that sound when she's getting fucked from behind, she thinks she does. A twinge goes down to her cunt, that little ache, signaling the need to be filled by something thick. She'd get Mr Wrong over later, much later, she needed to get fucked first, properly fucked, well she was going to have to, if she was going to entertain Mr Wrong this evening.

"Lez go, Bally Dancer. Fuck its freezin, lez trot," Crystal jogged a few steps, walked and jogged on again. Bally was close on her heel just a little to her left. They were over-taking everyone. Within six minutes they were coming up the familiar narrow staircase, the familiar smell greeted and they followed the same procedure they always did. Neither of them spoke, there was no point. Bally sat gently in her armchair, the heating was on full blast, she wasn't cold. Crack cocaine, in little balls looked at her from the table, Crystal saw her and put all 20 of them in the little tin black box that was on the TV. Then she passed her the tin, as Ballys heart started thumping, the anticipation was glorious, the excitement thrilling…fuck it felt so good and she hadn't even smoked any of it yet. Unwrap, flick, flick with their clippers, mmmm fuck that was so good, so very, very good.

"I wanna fuck Pete," Bally's voice was clear and to the point.

"Yeah, that was sort of embarrassin'ly obvious, to everyone apart from you earlier. So you didn't clock, or choose to ignore the bit where he ran out the door, screamin' get that fuckin deranged Irish bint off me," Crystal's 'Pete' impersonation was very good.

"Did he fuck, anyway who gives a shit, what he wants? I said I wanted to fuck him; he doesn't have to be willing. Actually I don't wanna fuck him, maybe just suck him off a bit. I bet his dicks like rock hard and massive and all angry and veiny. I bet he's the sort that fucks your mouth." Bally inhaled deeply, "I bet it fuckin stinks."

"Ok Bally Dancer, wot we got 'ere is the 'I want you to suck it' vs the 'I want to fuck your mouth', 'cause generally speaking, the male falls into one or the other category. It's difficult to tell with Pete, 'cause he's a bit of a dark horse and his movement is always fluid, so you don't get any indication of the ride he's gonna give the back of your throat. You know the jerky types."

Bally nodded sagely, laughing, "But you know its

meaty, hard, very hard and meaty. You know if you bit down it would be like fuckin granite."

"For fucks sake, fan yourself girl (all done in Pete voice). I wanna take my time and lick ya," (more Pete voice). Crystal flicks her tongue through her fingers licking them slowly. "I know it's turning you on girl, everything is turning you on, is yer pussy aching for some Pete Meat?"

"Yeah, anyway I've got Mr Wrong popping over later and I'll get on my knees and close my eyes and swap Mr Wrong's cock for Meaty Pete's; it should work as long as I've done enough brown, go into my method acting aura and I keep my eyes closed." Haha the girls scream with laughter... they were rolling.

Flick, flick their lighters go. Tick tock, the little travel clock goes beside the bed. Time does not stand still.

8 hours later - early Saturday morning.

"Adam is the original dull male...discuss?" both Bally and Crystal were in exactly the same places they'd been in for the best part of a day now. Bally's voice was slightly slurred and her eyes were droopy, she was pretty fucked, they both were.

"Bally 'oo the fuck you talkin' 'bout?"

"Adam the first male...Eve's sidekick."

"Oh yeah Adam, the dullest man on the planet…"

"Exactly Miss Cut Above the Rest Crystal, Eve on the other hand, is the original anarchist, every invention and discovery in the world starts with her. When she bit into that apple who could have predicted Vivienne Westwood would follow? If they weren't shamed into wearing clothes we'd be sitting here in the buff. Do you think God knows how to cut cloth like that? Fold fabrics? Er I don't think so!"

"Apple, tha' company 'as a bitten apple logo like the original sin. Mate, I think they're drawin' attention to 'ow fuckin sinful the cost of their chargers are…agree? Haha I suppose you're gonna tell me that's all our Eve's doin' as well?"

"Yes my friend I am," Bally was on a roll, Crystal loved her, truly loved her when she was like this.

"Yep, they needed shelter, and they need it fast. Kicked out the Garden of Eden with only a few leaves, forward fast several thousand years and voila, you've got the Marriott Hotel chain. They needed subsistence and they got McDonalds, they got McFlurrys. They needed jobs and they got Dixons, they needed to spice up they're flagging sex lives and along came Ann Summers, where they could by a double ended dildo and both get off at the same time, together, as a couple."

"Fuck Adam, the spineless cunt, 'e let 'er take the

can for tha' apple," Crystal was getting into Bally's rhetoric.

"The origins of the weak, pathetic male, whilst Eve our heroine..."

"Bet she did der brawn as well," interjected Crystal

"...goes on to become the creator of all life...yes that's it, she is God, she creates life, life grows within her and we all stem from her, all of us girls. Whilst all man stems from is Adam..."

"Tha' explains Mista Wrong den." The girls piss themselves laughing. Crystal's never met Mr Wrong, but she's heard enough about him, all totally wankerish, she's crying with laughter.

"Eve gets to fuck Adam with a Mista Dick Realistic Dildo...would you fuck Mista Wrong with a Mista Dick Realistic Dildo? Let me rephrase that, 'ave you fucked Mista Wrong with a Mista Dick Realistic Dildo?"

With a slow smile Bally answers eloquently, "Do you not think I humiliate the man enough?"

"Yer do, yer do," Crystal wails, crying into her hands and collapsing over the sofa arm.

Flick flick, inhale, hold it, exhale...

7 hours later – early Saturday evening.

Mr Wrong's txt message pops up on the screen.

Nearly Thirteen Months

10 minutes

"Night night Bally dancer," Crystal pulls on her Artic outdoor wear, they hug goodbye. Bally looks fucked. Click the front door goes as she lets herself out.

Out on the street, her first intake of breath hurts, its dark, she whistles a cab in seconds, climbs in and flings herself onto the back seat.

"Where to love?"

She can see him eying her up in his mirror. He's incredibly unattractive.

"City Road, south of Old Street tube," she snaps, all her previous humour has fled, she's on the street now, on her own and no one takes the piss. She stares out the window.

"Right you are." He's seen her type before low class hooker with a big mouth, fuckin little slut talking to him like that. Bet she's got nice tits though. Bet she gets 'em fucked regularly.

The cabbie pulls up outside her block and she gets out and pays the fare. Hostility flickers between them. She enters her block quickly, no fumbling for keys and takes the stairs. Crystal never gets in a lift unless it's waiting, she's not the waiting type.

Her flat is an enormous one bed, with gigantic floor to ceiling windows. There's a huge open plan kitchen, which is decked out with all the latest appliances. Not that she needs them as she only ever uses her Nutri Bullet. She never eats solids in the flat, nothing at all and never drinks anything apart from alcohol, bottled water and her Nutri Bullet juices. The fridge needs its own postcode, it's spacious. The freezer still has the plastic seals across the lower draws. The oven has never been used. She's lived there 2 years. It's a proper singleton's pad and up there on the 28th floor with its spectacular views over the city. It's her home. She feels safe there.

She smirks to herself thinking of her mate and the time they've had. She's never had a girlfriend before, in fact she hasn't had any friends before. Oh yes there's always been loads of acquaintances, but Crystal never opened up to any of them. Her previous life did not invite the most normal of relationships. Whilst her school friends were chatting round the breakfast table with their families before school, she was cleaning up the trail of vomit left by her junkie mother, who could barely cope with herself let alone her super intelligent daughter.

Her mother was a brass of the lowest kind, she flipped tricks wherever she could for drink and drugs. But she loved her daughter and Crystal knew that. It was her mother that had given her the nickname Crystal, when she was a baby, she had always known she was a cut above the rest.

These two women respected each other's choices and never judged, for all Crystal's Mum's faults she did her best with the tools she had and Crystal stood by her.

Crystal stood and admired her reflection in the mirror that covered one whole wall to the right of the kitchen. She was beautiful, she knew that. Her ash blonde wavy hair, that was now slightly tangled and messy, made her look even sexier, she thought. It skimmed down her across her shoulder blades and ended in V in the middle of her spine. She always wore black. Her black vest and tight black jeans, highlighted a figure that new know body fat. She didn't exercise, she just didn't eat much. At 5ft 9 she was tall, but not overtly, her broad shoulders and high waist made her long slim legs look magnificent. She knew she looked good. She felt in control and at 34 she had never been better. Her business was thriving, just as she was. Her motivational workshops were in serious demand and she could net thousands in a day. There wasn't anyone that didn't want to be like her, look like her. Her green eyes sparkled back at her, well that was her perception, as she was properly off her nut. Time to go to sleep. Two Zoplicone and 10mg Diazapam washed down with 500ml of Evian. Quick shower, wash hair, brush teeth and she was in bed within 20 minutes. It was 9.30pm Saturday night.

As always on the Zoplicone, her dreams were

vivid. Her mum taking her to West Wittering beach on their own, in the neighbour's gold Ford Cortina. She could feel the shingle beach and the warm sunshine, her hair whipped her face, it had been windy. She'd eaten ice creams and hot dogs all day from the van. Her mum smoked cigarettes and sipped from a flask that she knew had neat vodka in it. She could smell the vodka and the sea. They'd driven back laughing and joking and were singing 'Hit Me With Your Rhythm Stick' when they pulled into the flats.

Smithy her mums pimp had been waiting. She could feel the fear rise in the car. He waited for her Mum to get out the car. Crystal had been nine, it was her birthday, her mum told her to get out the car and go into the flat. Her Mum's voice was pleading, she was scared. Crystal didn't get out the car, she was hot and her thighs stuck to the seat. She watched Smithy punch her mum straight in the stomach and her mum drop to the floor on her knees. The tarmac was rough, she was wearing a skirt, Crystal thought she'd have nasty bruises on her knees after that. Then Smithy got his thin long dick out and pissed on her mother. She crouched with her hands over her head with the piss streaming and splattering off her. It seemed to go on forever, Crystal couldn't look away as she watched him shake his dick and saunter off, as the neighbours looked on at the sorry sight sight over their balconies. Getting out the car and could smell the

Nearly Thirteen Months

piss instantly as she walked up to her mum and tenderly put her arm around her. The two women made their way inside. The other residents looked away sadly. Cathy and her daughter were well liked.

She dreams of another Caroline, one who had a mother who was a house wife. A father that comes home every night and swings her around. All her toys are perfect and she has her friends over after school.

Sunday morning creeps into her bedroom slowly and wakes her gently. Her bed is enormous and the grey sheets only accentuate her beautiful skin. The sun streams across into the room, through the open blinds, its warm and she kicks back the duvet and basks in the weak rays. Ahh what a glorious morning she thinks and rolls over on to her back, smiling to herself as she falls back asleep.

Several hours later.

The suns gone, it's colder in the room Crystal wakes and feels the same Sunday feeling she's had all her life. What to do? What do people like her do on a Sunday? She makes a point of never working on Sunday. What do people do on a day off who have no friends or family? She does see her Mum regularly at least once a week but she always goes in the week, when she can be smartly dressed and hurrying back to work.

The day looms ahead. She'll get drunk, watch movies and play songs on Spotify, it's what she always does. But first she's got to eat, she's starving. Pulling on an immaculate pair of tracksuit bottoms and obligatory vest top, she never wears a bra, there's no point. She makes her way to the kitchen and gets juicing. And then its brush teeth, pull hair into pony tail, stuff herself back into more Artic wear and she's out the door leaping down the stairs.

As Crystal has no real friends and Bally rarely eats, she invariably finds herself in restaurants on her own. She gets the cabbie to take her down Brewer Street and says a quick hello to the staff as she eases herself onto a bar stool at the window of Randall & Aubin. She's been coming here for years and she knows she'll be left alone. A glass of Champagne is placed in front of her and within 10mins she's already slurped down 6 native oysters, followed by chips and lobster and several more glasses of Champagne. She doesn't linger and she's not even tipsy. She feels that aching Sunday feeling again, plasters a smile on and sets off for home.

By the time she gets back she's only killed an hour and a half. Once home, she gets the Stolychnia out the freezer and pours herself a decent measure. It's cold and syrupy, the hit buzzes her insides. Then she has another and another. Flipping open her laptop she opens Spotify. She's gonna get drunk and go into fantasy world, she's going to go as far

Nearly Thirteen Months

away from herself as she can. She's going to block her reality, quell the fear rising in her. No good comes of realising the fear.

Pulling of her top off, she looks at her body in the mirror, traces a line with her finger from the dip in her throat down to her crutch. Holding it tight, she yanks at it hard. Spotify is playing the Yeah Yeah Yeah's song Zero. Too masturbate or not too masturbate? She looks at herself in the eye and sees nothing. Nothing behind the façade. Nothing behind the beautifully shaped eyebrows and they are spectacular, thick tapered, honey brown and shiny. Sauntering into the kitchen singing, hips swinging to the beat she licks her lips and wonders what to drink next. Mr Justerini and his mate Brooks wink at her from the kitchen counter. She pours another wobbly measure in a small neat tumbler. It's sweet and warm and harsh, everything you could want in a beverage. Her head starts to buzz, she likes the buzz. Back to Spotify for a Black Eyed Peas session...fuck it let's dance together, let's dance in front of thousands, her head spins, she's on top, fans cheering. Dance, bounce bounce, grind she knows she looks good, hair tumbling down out of its ponytail. Fuck she's sooo good. Glug glug, whiskey spills down her chin, she licks round her mouth facing the mirror, she's disgusting, she's a fucking animal...and she goes on and on and on.

She's drunk and tired and it's no wonder as she's

been flinging herself around for nearly 4 hours. The J & B lies empty in the bin. It's dark outside. Closing her laptop the silence is a relief. Evian time, she's already drank 3 litres today. She downs another 500ml and heads to bed its 5.30pm. She needs her rest. She knows the importance of eating and sleeping. You are what you eat? Fuck she'd be a mobile pharmacy if that was the case. Sleep comes quick after a few tablets, she swaps the Zopiclone for a Tramadol...inhale, exhale, inhale, exhale.

12 hours later - 5.20am Monday morning.

Crystal is bright eyed and clear headed. She leaps out of bed, jumps in the shower and washes everything vigorously. Her skin is raw from the scrubbing and very smooth as she oils herself with a very expensive body oil. Only last year she did the laser hair removal thing, money well spent as she oils between her legs and marvels at the smoothness of her lips and mound. Oil again, hmmm rub, she always liked rubbing herself it felt good. She never over rubbed her clit just went around it, she was aroused and horny. Slowly, slowly, one hand on her mound, the other round the back she loved the feeling of her arsehole clenching as she came. She rarely had sex, what she did was wank. Her head came forward, eyes half closed as she mentally went to where she needed to go. She rarely had sex as men didn't satisfy her, no human did. She only got off on dogs, she's always been that

Nearly Thirteen Months

way, ever since she could remember.

Her first sexual encounter had been with one of the neighbours dogs. She'd been about 12 years old. It was a mongrel about knee high grey, scruffy and whiskery. She can remember how his tongue felt as he slowly licked her hand and how she'd looked after him that day and let his nose nuzzle on the front of her knickers under her thin cotton dress. She pulled at her cunt, grabbing it in her fist, one leg up against the wall, she went hard and fast and in under a minute came with shuddering relief. She wiped her engorged gash, admiring its beauty in the floor to ceiling mirror.

A while back she'd told Bally about her deepest darkest little doggie secret, Bally had a way of getting the truth out of her. Bally's response had been, 'always had a thing for Great Danes, it's the bollocks hanging down on show, does it for me every time.' And that had been that, Bally knew her secret and accepted her for being sick in the head. Bally didn't see it like that though, she called it the will of the overtly confident. Sex was a big topic for Bally. You needed to fulfill your fantasies otherwise you could never be complete as a human being, as an individual. It amazed her how much she thought about Bally, her weedy, reedy friend. Bally was by far the most interesting person she had ever me.

Bally talked openly about paedophilia, without

disgust just the facts, another hot topic of hers. It amazed her how Bally could remove herself emotionally and detach herself from everyday life. She'd learnt a lot from her. She made herself a fresh juice, did a bit of a tidy, put on a face and was on the way to her office in Shoreditch. Cool and trendy hipster bollocks, all bollocks that paid well. TAXI!

3 MARCH

"Happiness in intelligent people is the rarest thing I know."

> The Garden of Eden, Ernest Hemingway

Bally's phone bleeped, a text. Gareth had just cancelled, he was very sorry, they'd have to reschedule. Gareth was her boss, Le Grand Fromage. *Yes!* She mouthed to the heavens, tipping her head back and laughing! She had not been looking forward to the meeting he had arranged a week ago. The sun shone down upon her, she had just swerved a major bollocking, she had been saved. Spring had arrived in the city of London and the world was a beautiful place. It was the middle of March and the season of rebirth and growth buzzed all around her. Feeling euphoric she trotted out of her shared office and straight down the corridor into the toilet. Natural euphoria although greatly appreciated was not to be relied upon and with that she popped two diazepam.

Perfect start to the perfect day.

Her phone buzzed again as she was coming out the toilet. It was Api the solicitor that gave her most of her work. Bally briefly wondered why she did this, if she needed to instruct a barrister she wouldn't pick herself. She took the call immediately, the Diazepam gave her inner strength, today she would be capable.

"Hey Happy, hows it hangin'?" Api aka Happy was everything that was good in the world, rolled into one rotund second generation Ghanaian. At 5ft 3 with her dark, dark brown skin, (she would have never made the cut on a Colgate advert) even if she did have the whitest teeth ever, Happy was a beautiful person. She was a radiator, she exuded warmth. Bally often had a strong urge to huddle next to her.

"Bally, you're a bad girl, you never return my calls."

Bally's internal dialogue 'what fuckin calls?'

"Sorry babe, you know how it gets."

"I got some interesting work, lets have a chat honey, when's good for you?"

"Happy are you local? I can do now."

"Yep, lets meet in the usual, I'll buy us breakfast."

Nearly Thirteen Months

The usual was a café round the corner on Leather Lane the only one left on the road that did breakfast without a salad on it.

Happy frowned as she put the phone down. That Bally girl needed some looking after, she was on a downward spiral, at this rate she would lose her job. If only she could see it herself, she'd maybe try and talk to her.

Ten minutes later Happy walked in. Bally had already ordered the bacon sandwiches and tea, plus a plate of chips. They hugged warmly, they like each other a lot. Happy tried to hide her shock at the woman in front of her. Bally looked like a corpse. Her hair was lank, her face pasty and her eyes were dead. She must have been 6 stone, if that. In comparison, Happy looked the picture of health. Bally felt her scrutiny and stepped back and started to apologise. The brekkie arrived, it broke the ice. Happy patted Bally's hand and smiled non-judgmentally. She'd recovered her composure from her initial shock of sitting across the table from one of the 'living dead.' They chatted about work and both ate hungrily, leaving the previous tension behind them. The food did Bally the world of good and she felt relaxed and comfortable, well the food and the diazepam. Happy talked about her life, her boyfriend, she was in love.

Happy was 33 and she'd been in a long term relationship, for a long time and all she wanted was her boyfriend to ask her for her hand. Bally was amazed at the simplicity of her life. She was slightly envious of Happy and her happiness. They laughed and joked, Happy's life was so easy. Everyone knew her boyfriend was mad about her and wanted to marry her, it was just a matter of time. They hugged goodbye a solid firm hug and Bally didn't want to let go.

"Bally honey, I'm always here for you, come see me whenever."

"I know that Haps, thanks a million, thanks for bearing with me and my horrid virus that I can't shift, I feel like shit."

The little lie was kept in place and respected by both parties as they went out the door and went their separate ways. Happy knew all about living little lies.

Early that morning...

"Happy, I'm outta here, have a wonderful day pumpkin," Happy's boyfriend Paulie planted a kiss on the top of her head (he was much taller than her, to be fair most people were) and was out the door in seconds.

Happy went into the bathroom she felt the twinge and sat down on the toilet and wiped herself.

The blood red tissue stared back at her. Sadness swamped her like a cloak, hanging so heavy on her shoulders. It hurts so much, it hurts so much; she clutched her heart and a few tears came, she allowed herself a sob. Her shoulders heaved under their tremendous weight and her breath puckered.

And then as sure as the passing of time more tears came. She was nothing, she had nothing. She sat, tears streaming down her face, body shaking. Oh the pain, how could anything hurt so much, all she wanted was a baby, that's all. Women, real women, got pregnant all the time, what was wrong with her, why wasn't she capable of having a child, what was wrong with her? Her womb contracted suddenly and jolted her forward, just another little reminder of her womb rejecting another egg. Another egg wasted being flushed down the pan – literally. She would never be a mother, a real woman. Her heart tightened, squeezing out one, two more sobs, a gulp. 'Breathe focus on calm breathing', she whispered to herself. 'That's it swallow it down, swallow down the pain, bite down on it hard.'

Getting up she put a Lilet in and washed her hands and face. She knew she was exhausted, another month down and she wasn't getting any younger. Popping a few Nurofen she smiled her smile that everyone loved her for and with a quick dab of makeup she was out the door as cheery as ever, or

Jane De Croos

so it would appear.

Why, was a blow job called a blow job? She had never blown on a dick, had Happy? Bally giggled to herself and still on a high from avoiding the dreaded Gareth bollocking, she decided to get higher. It was a weekday, Crystal didn't snort, gulp or sniff in the week, she was on her own. That right now was a very good feeling. Happy had made her feel a bit uncomfortable; she knew she didn't look good. Happy always had that ability to bore into her soul. Hmmmm she wondered if Happy knew or guessed about her drug use. Bally shrugged off her dark thoughts and headed for home. Yay day off!

Bally was getting annihilated, the one thing about doing gear with Crystal was it slowed her down. But on her own the smack was gouging her out and the only way to stay conscious was to have a lick on her crack pipe. And she went on and on and on. Flittering in and out of reality her imagination went something like this:

Interviewer: Regarding orgasms, how many times have you faked it to make him hurry up?

Answer: Most of the time.

Imagine what it must be like for all those men out there who think they're doing a good job. Who would tell them that the reason it's faked is to spare them trying to do it right. Could you imagine the endless questioning and trying to understand what turns us females on? And then the horror and disgust when they realise the truth. That the only reason we like it doggie style is that we can imagine it being his best mate, brother...haha Dad! All three taking it in turns. All three together, the Father, the Son and the Holy Spirit. The Holy Trinity. Or as De La Soul put it 'Me, myself and I'.

Imagine some bloke thinking he's a pussy ace, he's on Mastermind

"So David your specialist subject is flange, good luck." (a titter can be heard from the females in the audience, fuck this fruitcake is gonna need more than luck, the questions were compiled by a woman, oh dear here comes the car crash)

Q1: When a woman moans when you're performing oral sex, what does that mean?

A: that she's enjoying herself.

Wrong, that she wants you to hurry up.

Q2. When a woman says half way through sex, I want you to come on my tits, what does she mean?

A: That she'd like me to ejaculate on to her because that turns her on.

Wrong, what she means is she wants you to stop having intercourse and hurry up so she can go back to watching Catchphrase.

Q3: Why would a woman initiate sex?

A: Because she's turned on and wants to have sex.

Wrong, because she wants you to pay for her car insurance.

Q4: When a woman says she likes what you're doing, what does she mean?

A: That she's getting turned on by what I'm doing and wants me to do more of it.

Wrong, that what you did earlier was so awful, please don't do that again.

Q4: When a woman says she's not interested in sex anymore, what does she mean?

A: That women don't really have the same sex drive as men.

Wrong, she'd have no trouble taking it up the arse from Gary next door. but the thought of having to put out for you again is far too dull to contemplate.

Q5: How do you make a woman orgasm?

A: Through stimulation of her clitoris

Wrong, you leave the room.

Hahaha....

Many, many, hours later. Her alarm goes off.

Another dream, another vivid snapshot into… what was it into? Why was it happening now? Bally lay under the thick duvet shivering with cold. Her sweat smelt, she smelt. Was it just her warped mind, she couldn't really believe that she could ever think like this, have those sort of thoughts. She remembered her mum pulling her knickers to the side; she was in bed about 6 years old, younger she didn't know for sure, she didn't know anything for sure. It was at night she'd been asleep, her mum had woken her saying there was something wrong. Her fingers were sharp, her red nail varnish always perfect poking inside her, were her mother's fingers inside her vagina? She didn't know, she knew it hurt, it stung. Her mum said it would hurt, that she had hurt herself and that "mammy would kiss her better." She can remember her wet tongue, licking at her, licking her down in that private place, she didn't push her mum away could feel her wiry, over lacquered hair on the inside of her legs. She could smell her sweet perfume, the Dior one, it was disgusting. It was all over in seconds, tucked back up in bed her mum wiped her mouth with a red fingernail and pushed back her hair. She looked red in the face, flustered. Bally started to cry…was it really true? She didn't trust herself, she didn't know herself well enough, she didn't know anything anymore. Who the fuck was she, what had happened?

Bally had never got on with either of her parents.

Her mother had been overbearing and had ruled the family with a narrow sighted stupidity. Her father had let it happen and Bally had always felt she'd let her parents down, or that's how they made her feel. She avoided them as best she could, it hadn't crossed her mind that she didn't owe these two people anything and that she could cut all contact with them.

Pushing all thoughts to one side, she got out of bed showered quickly and was out the door dragging her wheelie suitcase stuffed with case notes behind her. Destination Marylebone, she'd get on a bus, it was cheaper. Safely in a seat she gazed at her reflection in the window. She didn't look that bad today, not great, but not like dying, massive improvement then. Reading the billboards, it was all shit, she saw a postcard sticking out of the window edge, it was white with the following black writing

"The best way out is always through." — Robert Frost

She read it again and then again...her initial thought had been get off the bus and go home, yeah that really would be 'the best way out.' Then something made her think of her mother, should she ask her? But ask her what? She tucked the post card into her bag and got off the bus. Show time and she'd need her don't fuck with me head on, she was not well briefed this morning, but liked the client and was feeling very confident. Thirty five minutes later she was outside having a fag on her own, she'd lost, again! Bleep bleep her phone went, it was Gareth rescheduling their little personal chit chat, aka her major bollocking, for being so frickin useless. The meet was set for tomorrow 9am, she felt like lying down and crying.

The day had been exhausting, all she wanted to do was phone Pete, but she had to stay cool for tomorrows meet. Which meant early to bed, with a few Tramadol to take away the chills. Whoever said 'tomorrow never comes' was a dick, because there it was first thing the next morning. She felt OK, she'd slept well thanks to a hefty dose of painkillers. She wasn't due in court till the day after, so planned to stay in chambers after her meet and look hard at it: ie. be seen to be behaving herself.

She washed and dressed with care which was very unlike her, but her life was depending upon it. Her blow dried pony tail shone in the badly lit flat and her clothes were all clean. She let out an audible sigh and thought 'out the door, pecker up, courage don't fail me.' In no time at all, it honestly felt like moments, she found herself gingerly climbing the steps to the big black front door and was chanting cancel, cancel, cancel, as the door swung open and there stood the very charming Gareth himself.

"Fuck Bally where did you spend the night? Up some ones arse?"

"Unfortunately not, I was at home all of last evening, on my own," Ballys reply was quick and good humoured, she was never one to take offense, and this was one of the reasons Gareth liked her.

"Entre mon petit poussin," Gareth held the door open as she ducked under his arm, she could smell Linx Africa. He guided her into one of the client rooms and sat her down before seating himself. He looked cool and collected. She was sweating profusely. Not one to mince his words Gareth opened the meet;

"What the fuck is going on?"

"Errrrrr" Bally's response was obviously not what was expected...

"Errrrrrrr, what the fuck does errrrrr mean, oh hang on a minute let me get someone to translate. What the fuck are you doing?" Gareth's voice was getting louder.

"Let me try and understand why someone I put in this Chambers wants to fuck me up the arse without an invite or a lubricant, I just don't get it?"

"Emmmmm" she wiped the back of her hand across her mouth her face was wet with sweat. She couldn't speak, there was no point she was fucked.

"Everyone has a sniff girl, you know that, but they don't come to work looking like a Twilight Saga extra and don't fuckin lose cases, all the fuckin cunting time, you fuckin' dipstick prat. This is a cunting job, not a fuckin holiday in the let's get fucked up park." His voice suddenly dropped over the last few offensive remarks.

"I'm tired of babysitting you, Bally you've got a month to get your shit together, that's it, one month from today. Our next meet is on 22 April and I will tell you then if you get to keep your job." He'd gone into exasperation mode, visibly so, as he held his hands up to the heavens.

Bally hung her head in shame, she needed a lick, she needed to be home and under the duvet, she needed to call Pete, she needed Crystal. She needed something which wasn't being provided in this small room with four upholstered chairs and old fashioned wallpaper. She needed a room which Gareth wasn't in. She was close to crying.

BANG! Gareth's hand hit the table, making her jump out of her sweaty skin.

"Fucks sake Bally you're fuckin' it up already. One month!" With that he jumped out of his chair, flung the door open leaving it swinging. She was left paralysed, she'd been rumbled, there was only one word to describe her situation...FUCK!

She was gonna have to pull herself together, she was gonna have to sort herself out and quick. No more weekday treat days. From today she was a reformed character, she was gonna be a hot shot

Criminal Barrister. This was it, last chance saloon. Time to pull her proverbial socks up. She needed some fresh air. Walking out on to the street she found herself heading home, she needed to be home, to rest and do some work from there. That's the plan just get home and take it one day at a time.

She walked up the grimy staircase, with the flimsy handrail. Her phone went bleep it was a message:

Happy: Honey what happened, heard Gareth blew his head gasket?

Fuck that was quick. She walked into her flat dumped her bag and dropped into the armchair. The little black box stared at her.

Bally: Yeah he sort of went nutz.

Happy: How u babe, u at work.

Bally: I'm ok, just home.

Happy: Home? Honey u need 2b in work, go back?

Bally: Will go tomoz.

Happy was starting to piss her off, she fingered the little black box

Happy: Bally u gotta do the right ting.

Bally: Gotta go, tnks 4 chat. Dnt worry xx

This was all so much bullshit, with that she

Nearly Thirteen Months

turned her phone off and opened the little black box. Heroin lay neatly folded in a piece of foil, she needed a little touch. Reaching under the sofa where the foil lived she pulled it out and tore off one piece, just one. Her tube was next to the box. Tap, tap on to the foil rectangle, tilt down, light and inhale all at the same time, let it run, run, run. This was no job for an amateur. Ahhhh the peace enveloped her, drew her in, comforted. She changed into her comfy clothes and settled on top of the duvet, bringing everything she needed, foil, little black box, lighter, pipe, ashtray, remote control.

The clock said midday.

She clicked the remote control, This Morning sprung up on the old screen. Another hit on the foil, hmmmm it was so lovely, all her worries faded away. She'd have one last day, no more stress, just one more day and then she'd definitely sort her shit out. She needed this, everything had been so fucked up recently, she was under so much pressure, all those shitty cases, work piling up, no frickin' money. Her mum, the dreams, the visions, fuck it was all too mad. She needed more gear, time for a little lick on her pipe. The ash was plentiful in the ashtray and her pipe only needed a quick change of top foil. Her heart quickened and her palms sweated lightly, she wiped them dry on the duvet. The build-up was incredible, the pure joy she was about to feel, flooded all her senses, literally drowned them in something so light and euphoric she could only smile at the bliss of it all. Yes that was it, it was pure bliss. She unwrapped one ball and opened it out laying it out on a magazine. She pinched off one large yellowy rock and stuck it on her pipe, on top of the ash, perfectly balanced and carefully brought the side of the bottle to her lips, mouth round one hole, finger over the other. Lighter poised she set the rock alight and inhaled, easy does it, nice and gently draw it in, let it fill the lungs, more, more, more and hold. Hold it. Hold it. Ahhhhh it's so pure, so fuckin perfect, so clear and exhale ahhhhhh so beautiful, so good to relax, feel so fuckin' good.

Time for a song, the CD player whirred, love smoking crack, feels so good. And then Bally did some more because everyone knows1 cracks so moreish and nothing tastes so good. Ohhh it's so very good, fuck it's so good. High, she was getting high, her mind flittered about, daydreams and fantasies old and new crashing upon the shores of pure bliss, smoothing away all the problems of the day, leaving everything behind. This was where she was truly happy, this is where she wanted to be, this was the best, it was amazing. Smiling to herself, she leant back and let the music, drugs and her imagination work their magic...yes it was pure bliss. As she daydreamed, reliving conversations...

"So why dan't we tell blokes we're sleep wit woz going on?"

"Darling what men do you sleep with?" Bally arches an eyebrow at her doggie loving friend and smiles.

"That's the reason I dan't, so wot 'bout you Bally why dan't you tell Mr Wrong?"

"What? Tell Mr Wrong about the secrets of woman? Why the fuck would I give him that most precious of gifts? Anyway he's too stupid to get it, he thinks he's a great lover."

"Nah..." Crystal's disbelief was unsure.

"Yes," Bally's confirmation was solid. "And I nearly killed him the other day."

"Wot for finkin' 'e's a great lover?"

"Haha...no what the fuck, of course not! No, I nearly killed him, with that phone directory, the one by the front door."

Crystal was familiar with the murder weapon in question; she'd tripped over it many times.

"Cryst it was awful," Crystals eyes widened, she was actually becoming rather concerned.

"He accidentally had an unscheduled sleepover. It was awful. I woke up in the AM with him next to me in my bed. There he was fast asleep like some fucked up nightmare gone wrong. I was awake and he's asleep and it's my flat. What the fuck!!! I had to put 'Operation Escape' into action."

"Op'ration Escape, not Op'ration Bump Him Off?" Crystal was keen to establish some normality...if that was at all possible.

"Sshhh and I'll tell you. I slip out from under the covers commando style, in more ways than one. Slide across the floor picking up a few items, wiggle into them in the hallway and I'm just about to get out the door and he wakes up. We literally eyeball each other for what feels like 10 hrs and then for some unknown reason I pick up the phone directory and hurl it at him and it hits him straight between the eyes and knocks him out sparko. And then I'm out the door and set up in the cafe opposite to keep a look out."

"Look owt? Look owt for fuckin wot mate?" Crystals beginning to think her mate's losing the plot.

"Mr Wrong, of course. I'm right there one seat from the window, I've got an uninterrupted view of my front door. And I wait, if he's not out in an hour I can presume he's dead. And if he is still alive he'll need to leave the flat and I'll know exactly when he goes so I can get back to where I live and stop being temporarily homeless."

"Ok..." Crystal said slowly, she was suddenly not so keen to hear the answer. "So...he did get up 'n go?"

"Yeah he was up and out in ten mins, but let me tell you mate, it was the longest ten mins I've ever done over a latte." And then they laughed, they both laughed without a care in the world and that made Bally smile to herself.

4 APRIL

Who is the third who walks always beside you?

> The Waste Land, T.S. Eliott

Pete eased down the street, not too fast, not too slow, nothing would make you take another look at him at long distance. His whole persona blended into the street, the pavement, his surroundings. Don't get me wrong he looked good, very good but he didn't stand out. He'd be impossible to describe, he looked 100% average bloke, one could say a fantastic attribute for a drug dealer. In fact, if drug dealing had been a career choice in 6th Form, his careers advisor would have matched him with it instantly.

Outside the looming Victorian gates of his daughters school, he paused momentarily looking up at the red brick building, the place had always looked more like a prison to him. Walking inside he was relaxed, purposeful and in control, Pete was always in control. The control was what made him sexy. Had he ever tripped up or gone the wrong way by mistake? It was doubtful.

Pete had 3 girls, Juniper who was a very mature 9, Pearl the creative one at 7 and Little Gracie who was the sweetest thing, at age 5. He started dealing when his wife of 8 years got up and left, emailing him from Mexico saying she was never coming back, that had all taken place 4 years ago. He'd always been ducking and diving, but as a single parent he needed childcare and that wasn't cheap and a job in which he could pick his own hours. He had never gone to look for his wife and never once emailed her back. He showed his eldest daughter the email at the time, read it out to her, said he loved them all and it was just him from now on. They understood, they were always close. Nobody mentioned her again.

Pete came from a lower middle-class family. He'd grown up in the suburbs of south London, in a large four bedroom terrace, on a pretty little tree lined street, with his brother, sister, mum and dad. It was just his parents now in the house they'd live in for nigh on 40 years. Nothing had changed, everything was the same as when he was a boy. Both his parents were civil servants and fully retired. They had also always been tight with money. They were cash rich and stingy, which had made Pete generous and gregarious. I suppose he could have thanked them for that, but he didn't.

Instead Pete, disliked his family immensely, he always had. As a boy he can remember despising his fathers' low level intellect and his mothers' mousey virtuosity. His brother and sister both younger, were both very straight, and both very dull, with jobs that reflected this. His brother John worked in IT and his sister Sarah in HR. Pete told his family he worked in security for very rich clients, which is sort of what he did before, hence the ability to get into high end drug dealing. His clients were bored and stupid, but most of all loaded. And the dollar kept rolling in. And boy did it roll in. Drugs were big business they always had been. Pete bought in bulk and distributed in secure and safe amounts. His fee was astronomical, but he was cautious and tidy. The money was so good it was difficult to give up, but he had a plan and for that he'd need capital.

Pete wanted a top class retreat, no TV, no outside interference, peace and tranquillity. What Pete wanted was bliss and for that he was going to have to get out of London and go abroad. Southern Europe, the Med, warm, relaxed and most of all away from his South London roots. He'd partially reinvented himself already by ignoring his family; he wouldn't have any trouble picking up sticks with his little ladies. He was on his way.

Upon entering the school, he was surrounded by image after image of children's rubbish drawings, let's be honest here, they were all shite. He smiled briefly at his own humour, heading for the office. It wasn't his first time. The Receptionist – what most men would call dishy blonde and what Pete would call a little slut, welcomed him in and told him to take a seat. "Mr Manners the head's a bit delayed, I'll tell her you're here," she had that silly girl vocal that made her sound even more stupid than she was. Pete cringed discreetly, dropped himself rather too quickly in a soft looking, but actually very hard chair, stifled an ouch and focused on the wall.

Black horse

Magic horse

Carry me away

      By Jola, 6 years old

Never a truer word written he thought, at least there's one kid in this dump with some talent (excl. his daughters, of course).

The Receptionist took off down the corridor, her first destination was to the staff room and hoped to find at least one female staff member. She was in luck as the chemistry and art teachers were both on the sofa, as she barged through the door.

"Junipers Dad's here, OH MY FREAKING GOD, MY

CLITS ON FIRE," Pete had the sort of popularity with the female staff that would have made Robbie Williams look like the tea lady. The teachers suddenly came out of their over worked, under paid and most of all, treated like shit stupor and turned to face Bev, who had no problem shrieking...

"OH MY GOD, HE WALKED STRAIGHT TOWARDS ME WITH THOSE ICE BLUE EYES, I FUCKIN' NEARLY CUM RIGHT THERE ON THE CARPET."

Jessie the art teacher licked her lips and made a rather crude dick swallowing face by holding one clenched fist up to her open mouth, whilst her other hand was positioned at the back of her head bobbing it up and down. She was also making lots of gagging noises. Her sound effects were pretty realistic, thought Bev and she was just about to point this out when a hard slap to the thigh from the chemistry teacher stopped Jessie's bobbing and gargling.

"GOTTA RAINBOW DASH," screeched Bev and bolted out the door. Next destination – Head Mistresses Office – Mrs Cunnings aka Mrs Lemon Cuntings. Rumour had it she slept her way to the top because she had no skills in any other area whatsoever. But Bev and the rest of the staff closest to her seriously doubted that, as Mrs Cunnings it was presumed had the sort of cunt that not even the MRSA bug could survive in. It was what one would call a hostile environment.

Rat tat tat went Bev on the glass pane, which shuddered in its frame. The Head looked up and prayed silently that the intercom phone system would be fixed very soon so she could minimalise the contact she was forced to have with Bawdy Bev the Banshee. Fuck the woman looked like a road accident involving a small plump animal and a cast iron bumper.

"Come in Bev," she spoke without emotion.

"Junipers dad's here," she panted, her offensive voice smashing through the serenity of the small office like a sledge hammer.

"Bring him in will you Bev. Thank you."

Smash! The door crashed shut as Bev spun round on a rather swollen ankle and took off. Doesn't that twit ever walk anywhere mumbled Mrs Cunnings to herself and pulled out Junipers file.

Pete sat at ease in the chair opposite as Mrs Cunnings looked up from the file and began.

"Thank you Mr Manners for coming in, as I discussed briefly on the phone, I would like to talk to you about Juniper," not a flinch thought Mrs Cunnings, this man was unnervingly calm. Did he not ever falter? Well we'll see how he takes this.

"Juniper as I'm sure you're aware is doing very

well here." Not even a smile, a nod, acknowledgement, nothing…"She's really quite exceptional," she added quickly. Oh dear she was starting to ramble, get into a panic.

"We would like to place her on the The Gifted & Academic Programme," Mrs Cunnings leaned back waiting for the joy to spread across this man's face…and she waited. Not even a flicker, no leaning forward, no gasp, no nothing. The man was an impenetrable wall of ice.

Leaning forward she continued eagerly,"The program is a government scheme that aims to enhance the educational development of students between the ages of 4 and 19. Juniper starts secondary next academic year and I think she should apply for a scholarship to one of the top private schools. Her mathematic ability is literally outstanding. You must be terribly proud." And breath, shit he wasn't even blinking, what the fuck was wrong with this man. She could feel the perspiration wet under her armpits. She inhaled deeply through her nose, had she started to smell?

"Mrs Cunnings is there anything further you'd like to discuss?" His voice was coarse, masculine, inviting. She wanted to pour her heart out, tell him how much she missed a man's touch, a real man's caress, had she'd even ever had one? She reflected rather painfully.

Pete saw sorrow, briefly cross her face and had an understanding of what had made her so sad, this brittle and controlling woman. He felt no pity. He'd seen her type before. His wife Maria had been like this, horribly manipulative and righteous. He can remember doing everything to appease her, as nothing was ever good enough. She found continual fault in everything he did. Miss Black and Fuckin' Cunting White. Why he always did things for everyone else? Why he never had time for her? How he didn't care? But that wasn't the case, he had liked his wife, provided for her. And all she did was fuckin' moan at him. Tell him what to do and how to do it. He spent many years avoiding her questioning, she was his wife-- didn't she know her place? When she had left, after the shock had subsided, a great sense of relief had washed over him, that bitch was dead to him. The household would now be doing it his way, as they should have been doing all along. His ex was an idiot for even thinking her opinion counted.

"Er no" she stuttered. What! He wasn't going to ask her anything? Obviously not, as he got up, nodded slightly in her direction and walked out the door, closing it silently behind him. Bev could learn a lot from this man. Ooooh she felt that familiar twinge, damn it the man made her fanny ache for a fuck.

Pete was out of the door with such speed that Bev didn't stand a chance with her pre planned ambush. She sulkily watched the man of everyones' dreams walk with that 'Men in Black' gait right out the gates. Bollocks!

Once on the street, he thought for the first time about what The Head had just said and a big smile ripped across his face. Go on little Juno, she was a proper little number, well done her. It didn't concern him that he had not participated in usual or what society would call, normal inquisitive behaviour in the meeting. He never gave anything away, especially not to a woman, if you wanted it, you paid.

Right, back to work and he was on his way to see young Bally. Pete liked Bally she was different from other women, she was funny and clever, but the girl was on the edge, he'd seen it all before.

Yeah he'd seen it all before and she was a classic case. And as he walked into the cafe on Brewer Street, he clocked her immediately, sitting up against the 1970's coffee machine. It was a warmish day and she was wrapped in her enormous fur collared coat which made her look even more frail. She was a junkie, her look defined her now and it was as plain as the nose on your face to everyone apart from her. She looked up at him with her dead eyes and he saw her pain. And for the first time in his life as a dealer he felt responsible. Was that the word? Yes he felt responsible. Instead of doing anything worthwhile he was peddling shit to desperate human beings. He was making money out of their fear, turning a profit because they had no hope. His mind followed a path of righteousness. He had made a decision. And the decision he made right then, would be the right one. He had enough money and it was time to put his plan into action.

"How's my Bally Dancer?" He sat down, not waiting for her to answer.

"Bally sweetheart," his voice was cool and melodic it soothed her, it was like moisturising your face after a day in the sun. Her lips were dry, she didn't lick them, she knew it wouldn't help, her skin was dry. She had a vaseline lip balm in her pocket and wanted to smear it all over herself.

"Bally, this is the last drop." Bally sat up, like a child who had just been told off. Her mouth opened, but she had no saliva and her voice didn't work properly. She mouthed "What", but it came out as "wro." She tried to say something else, but was interrupted by two teas. Pete put two sugars in Bally's and slid it over to her side. She was obviously in shock. He handed her the little gift bag, it was lilac and the name tag said Happy Birthday Sally.

Everything was going in slow motion, like when you're in a car accident. The world was slowing down, it was about to stop spinning, which meant she was moments from falling off. The gift bag smelt funny and she instantly felt sick, she was always feeling sick these days. Sipping her tea, she needed all the strength she could muster, she nodded her understanding. What she really wanted to do was cry out loud and beg him to continue. But she knew it was over. She'd lost her dealer. Fuck she'd lost her dealer. She began to tremble, fuck she needed to get home quick. She needed to get home and close the door. Close the door tight shut and never come out again. Fuck she didn't have a dealer anymore, what she had on her was it! She'd have to go out and score. Fuck! Fuck! Fuck!

Pete placed his hand over hers and squeezed, she couldn't maintain eye contact. She'd never see him again. He'd collect the money off Crystal and that would be that. And then he was actually gone. He hadn't touched his tea. Gino came over with a bacon sandwich and left it on the vacant seat side of the table. Wordless. No words. She thanked Gino, hauled herself out of the grey plastic chair and walked unsteadily to the door. Pete must have paid the bill, she hadn't seen him do it. Only one minute ago, she was living her life, how she wanted. Now she couldn't even think about the end of the week. And the end of the week was coming.

Pete stopped two corners down from the cafe and leaned his back against the wall of an office block. Looking up he could see a bit of the blue sky, there it was behind all the grey clouds. Breathing in the city air, he took in what he'd just done. He's made his decision he was out of the game and wow he felt good. It was as if his whole body had become lighter, if he wanted to right now he could fly. Wow what a feeling, happiness saturated his body, his face, his smile. That was it, he was done. He was free. They were leaving London, all was well apart from a tiny little niggling feeling about Bally, she had shown him the right way, what path to take and he was abandoning her. Shit if only she wasn't such a junkie, he would get involved, he knew he could and would. Pushing the uneasy feeling about Bally out the way he cleared his mind to debate his next moves. He was excited.

Now to wrap things up and don't forget, this is Pete were talking about here. His exit strategy was already a carefully constructed plan. He bumped his back off the wall, the way cool teenagers did in films and practically bounced down the pavement, arms swinging. The first day of the exit strategy, the wheels were in motion, the machine had begun to turn. Don't think just do. Looking up at the sky once more, focusing on the tiny little bit of blue he thanked the universe whole heartedly for keeping him safe. He was very nearly clear, just a little bit more to go.

Bally's phone rang in her pocket, she didn't even bother to look at it. She needed to get some gear in her, she needed to feel safe. One quick stop at the local shop for a clipper, some foil, 10 Marlborough Lights and a 2 litre bottle of Evian and she'd be home. She felt slightly paranoid paying for her supplies as the shop keeper, who knew her well, asked her how she was? Did he know? And why did she even care?

What she bought was her business. Sweat trickled down her back as she climbed the stairs, she was nearly home. She would be OK in 5 minutes. Her stomach cramped suddenly, racing to the toilet the diarrhea came quick followed by the greeny yellowy bile of her stomach. Luckily, the never used tiny tin dustbin was in there, with a handy plastic bag in it. There is a God after all she thought briefly, otherwise it could have been messy. This joke made her smile, or was it the relief? Phew that felt loads better, she was ready now.

It was Thursday at 4pm, the grotty flat was dark and the damp stained ceiling was getting worse. Or was it? She couldn't remember, she didn't care. The hit from the crack was so good. Ahhhhh! I love again, I'm happy, I'm content, I'm complete. Her phone rang again, she could answer it now she was better. It was work.

Bally - "Hello work."

Junior Clerk - "Bally, I've got something for you, domestic, she's knocking seven bells out of him,

Nearly Thirteen Months

and she's done him over pretty good this time, stitches, bruises the lot along with nice photographic evidence backed up with a hefty hospital report of him looking like a cheap Hungarian tit job. Where are you?"

Bally - "Home, but I errrr...."

Junior Clerk - "Gareth said if I heard you say 'er' I was to say 'one month cunt face' fuck knows what that means. Anyway, I'm biking it round now. Ciao for now."

Bally - "Ciao for...." The phone went dead.

'Errrr' did she say that a lot? Fuck Gareth, he's the cunt...she'd show him!

An hour later she had the case on her lap and was flicking through the pages, whilst taking deep medicinal draughts on her crack pipe. This one would be a doddle, time for a little vodka perhaps?

She put herself to bed at a decent hour, congratulating herself for laying off the brown. Maybe she would start just doing it on weekends. Yeah, cut right down and focus on work. Or not at all? No dealer, remember? The two DF118's infused with her mind taking away all the worry, ssssh, sssshh, ssshhh, they went and she fell into a glorious deep sleep. The type only medication could induce.

Morning the birds chirped, just like in Cinderella. She must be dreaming, but what a fantastic dream a rotund, blue tit was talking to her, wakey, wakey it said, rise and shine. What was supposed to shine? She got up and showered, and peered at herself in the small mirror. Not her face by all accounts which had taken on a deathly pallor and pasty sheen. She attempted to reduce the sheen with a whitish Max Factor powder. It wasn't Max Factor's fault, the sheen stayed and was now happily glowing from the protective base of about 7000g of heavy duty makeup.

Her phone said 9am and informed her that Mr Wrong had made several enquiries the previous evening:

11.37pm

B u tried to kill me?

11.42pm

Who cares... love ur flange. jst wanna b inside ya.

11.44pm

Wanna b in yer knicker good book.

1.51am

cum in my muth

Oh dear he'd obviously gotten slightly over refreshed. Her fanny sent a rapid message to her brain, saying 'get his cock and his tongue over here right now, his thick yellowy disgusting tongue...'

she deleted the message. Mr Wrong was a wanker and she was on the straight and narrow. Arghhhh her hand slipped onto her mound, as she dropped to the mattress and promptly masturbated for all of 6 seconds. OOOh that was good, just the thought of some big cock inside her made her cum. Shuddering twice she was back on her feet and got quickly dressed as she toyed with the idea of staying in and wanking all day. Naughty, naughty, case to win and with that she was bagged up and out on the street in minutes.

Picking up a coffee she was on the bus minus her big coat, it was far too warm for that, even though she felt horribly exposed and vulnerable without it. Shuddering she wondered what the day had in store for her, then she remembered the severity of the last meet she had with Pete. It was like forgetting someone had died and going to phone them and having to relive the horror of them not being there ever again. Her bowels tightened, in a threatening manner. This was serious. OK Option 1, find another dealer fast, scoring on the street was a serious headache. Dirty drugs and scummy dealers it was riddled with problems, such as getting arrested and being struck off from the Bar. Or Option 2, clean up her act and become an amazing Barrister, an amazing drug free Barrister. Allah, or whoever it was that's was running the show nowadays has just opened a door for her to walk right through if she wanted. She was going to take it.

She was gonna get clean, this was just the beginning of the rest of her life. That was the answer. She was being given an amazing opportunity to go straight. The gods had intervened. She felt a surge of purposefulness.

Dragging her wheelie suitcase up the Court steps, she began to weaken. Her head throbbed as she barely managed to open the huge doors, go through security and stagger to a bench to recuperate before her client sat heavily next to her. He had recovered from his battering and now just looked like a revolting thug. He introduced himself with a horrid Brummy accent, blimey no wonder his missus wanted to punch his lights out. She had a similar desire herself and had only just met him. She tapped one low heeled shoe on the tiled floor and contemplated cracking his skull with it. Hmmmm and then she could have a drink to celebrate.

As the Judge declared the accused innocent in a case of deliberate provocation, Bally sat motionless. She had hardly known what was going on. Had she been given the right notes? She walked out apologising briefly to her client and headed straight to the toilets and the last cubicle. Sitting down on the lid, she pulled mindlessly at a postcard poking out the side pocket of her wheelie bag...

"The best way out is always through." — Robert

Frost

'Is it really Robert' she thought to herself. It was the 10th of April, 12 days to go till Gareth fucked her up the arse without a lubricant let alone a frickin' invite. She could shoot herself, get a gun and blow her head off? It would be kinder. Taking a few Diazapam she stayed seated on the toilet and waited. She didn't have to wait long. Ten minutes later the world was a much better place. She could carry on. Its was Friday it was the weekend.

She let Crystal in and they stood in the little damp room in silence for what felt like an uncomfortably long time. Crystal could smell neat vodka she spoke first; her voice was steady and sounded well-rehearsed.

"I'm goin' clean. Saw Pete for the last time."

Bally kept her own council.

"I don't wanna be fucked in the 'ead no more."

More silence, it had got to a point that it was starting to make a noise. A harsh white noise, slamming into every free space in the tiny hovel they stood in.

Bally slumped into her chair and looked up at her friend with her shinny ponytail and exquisite bone structure. Crystal's makeup was immaculate. Bally in comparison looked like a concentration camp survivor.

"What are we saying here? It's time to jack out the world of bubble and enter the harsh cold bucket of reality." As she spoke the words, she was somehow not convinced. Her eyes darted over to the little black box, Crystal tracked her eye movement. They both looked away, reading each other's minds. They didn't need an excuse; they knew how it was going to go.

Crystal picked up the little black box and kneeling before Bally opened it as if showing her a rare cut diamond. She proposed a last time...words, language, dialogue were unnecessary. The room was fully charged with the excitement of the forbidden. Armed with foil, cigarettes, lighters, pipes, pins, Evian they took up position. And then they both had their first lick on their own pipes. And this is how their night went:

Ohhhh nothing ever tasted so good. Fuck it was sooooo good! FUCK!!! Bally could read Crystals thoughts, she knew, they smiled up at each other. Love surrounded them, enveloped them within its protective layer. They were everything to each other. Joy, intense joy seeped from their very pores. Their bond of understanding strengthened with every lick. Powerful and all complete. No one would ever come close to this. No one.

The clock tick tocked its mantra by the mattress reminding no one that it was 10.30pm.

And they got high and they drank shots and they, spliffed and they got high some more.

And they talked and talked and talked:

"What shall we do together now that we're not gonna be getting wankered anymore?" Bally was laughing out loud at her own humour, knowing that she could run a very long way with this one.

"Yeah good idea Bally, lets plan some activities?"

"Did you know I did book binding at school and was really good at it?" Bally was quick of the pace and was speaking in her legal voice.

"No I fuckin didn't mate, you must 'ave forgot ta tell me that story... and for that I can only fank our dear, dear close friend Alzehimers."

"I'd like to revisit that, I'd like to explore that craft further. Would you be interested? Obviously you'll want to think about it, I mean you can't make such a life changing decision without careful consideration?"

"Nah to book binding, too dangerous mate, ev'r 'ad a paper cut?" Crystal had given her answer. And how they laughed. But our girl was not to be put off.

"Ok book binding has its downside, but that's what makes it exciting eh? OK how about crochet?"

"Don't really 'ave the weather for it, but I do like knocking balls 'bout."

"That's fuckin' crocket you rrrrrrrrrrrrretard." They were rolling around eyes watering, Crystal looking like she was gonna pee herself. And they went on and on.

Tick tock, tick tock, 2am. Time waits for no one.

They were smoking Charas, it was beautiful, it made the world sparkle. Little one skinners, one for me one for you. And they talked and they laughed.

"I've jacked in Mr Wrong."

Crystal smiled at her friend "I bet that was 'ard."

"Fuck you, I loved that man," Bally struggled with sincerity, when she said the word 'love' it came out all wrong.

Crystal was all over her, "You twat you can't even say it. Go on give it another go, relax breath, no rush...I'm gonna have to hurry ya! Go on say it again, say 'I love that man' just pretend, or try ta pretend."

"Ok here goes...'I love that man.' Oh my days, what's going wrong? Why can't I say that?" Bally's vocals pitched all over the place.

"Give it up sweeth'art, itz not yer word, use

somefink else."

"What like, hate?" Bally couldn't help herself, as she said the word 'hate' she arched her thin eyebrows.

"Yay..well done that's loads better, loads more natural, more you."

"Yep you're right it's just so much more me. I need to be more negative, I feel it's really helping with understanding myself." Bally was grave and in therapist mode.

"Mate with those skills you could get a really good job in the service industry, on an 'elp desk? Shit you're totally wasted in yer field."

"Slogan T-shirts, HATE MORE – LOVE LESS."

"Right what's your marketing budget? I feel we've got something here," Crystal's affected media mogul impression, was superb. And they continued, talking shite, on and on and on. Bally uncurled the foil, it was time to come down.

Tick, tock, tick, tock.

Crystal got up to leave it was 10.45am on Saturday morning. The smell of burning heroin filled the air, it smelt good. Out on the street it was wet and drizzly, she wrapped her coat tight around her and felt a great sadness wash over her. She knew she couldn't go on like this. Would she ever see Bally again? Bally was in a right two and eight, she was going down and Crystal didn't like the pull on her. She was no fool this girl and knew she could not help her friend. Crystal knew that it was gonna get very dark for Miss Casey for a long time before it got better, if it ever did. Crystal was gonna jump ship.

5 MAY

With all sweet things it passed away,

And left me old, and cold, and grey

> May, Christina Rossetti

This year May Day heralded no triumphant joy for Bally, not that it ever had. She sat slumped in the armchair in her grotty, damp riddled flat and actually prayed for divine intervention. Her life had fallen apart, she had unravelled, she had been rumbled, she had nothing. She'd gone from criminal barrister at mediocre London Chambers to unemployed junkie fuck up, in under 2 weeks. And it was not a nice feeling. She felt sick, she felt like throwing up.

Her meeting with Gareth at 8am on the 21 April, had taken place on the street outside Chambers. They had stood beside a railing which Bally had clung to for both physical and emotional support.

"Morning Gareth, hows everything with you?" Her

pseudo upbeat delivery had come out a bit high pitched and what with the fake smile and attempted energy spurt, she had come across like some demented children's presenter. Gareth, not one to mince his words got straight to the point.

"I don't want to see you for three months, you will be welcomed back with open arms if you a) manage to get your drug usage under control b) stop looking like a fuckin cunting corpse."

'Errrrrrr"

"And you stop saying 'errrrrrrr'."

Bally clamped her mouth shut...did she always 'errrrr' and if so how long had she been doing it for? What was Gareth saying, she felt herself slipping.

"You could be really good Bally, really good, for fucks sake, get your shit together. We see each other in 3 months. Get some help, you need help, look at the fuckin' state of you. Have you even got a mirror at home? We look after our own here and that's why you're not getting the sack. I've got some money for you to tide you over for the summer, I'll have it banked to you." Gareth's tone was in his usual exasperation mode, in fact he looked for one moment quite kindly.

"Eeee," she squeaked. It was definitely not an 'errrrrrrr' more like a slow and controlled exhalation. She felt close to collapse, how had it come to this?

"Bally look at this as an opportunity. An opportunity to learn to say proper words, instead of fucked up weird noises, and get a tan...oh yeah and kick a fuckin', cunting drug habit. It's the summer, take time to get some fresh air." Gareth's kindly expression had been rapidly replaced with his usual fucked off one, maybe she had imagined the doting parent look? Was she hallucinating? Fuck she was losing her mind, no she wasn't, it was worse, she was losing her job. Fuck...she'd...lost...her...job. Everything had gone staccato. How could she ever go back, not now they all knew about her drug use. Her world had gone into 'bullet points.'

- bye
- bye
- job
- bye
- bye
- career

Gareth walked away and she didn't turn round, just continued to hold on to the railings. An "errrrrrrrrrr" seeped out of her pursed lips. What did it matter now...to errrr or not to errrr was no longer relevant; she'd just lost her fuckin', cunting job. And then the pit of despair got deeper, she'd have to tell her mum. No she wouldn't, she'd come back in three months fit and ready to be the best she could be. She'd get her job back, she'd have an amazing career as a top criminal barrister. She was gonna clean up her act, but first she needed to self-medicate. She needed to take stock. She needed to collapse somewhere private.

No job, oh yeah and no fuckin dealer either. She went home, tanked up on some Tramadol and was just gonna have to wait until the junkies came out of hibernation to go and score. They'd know who to use and junkies always sorted you out with dealers, it was what they did. In fact, they had an encyclopedic knowledge of street dealers and runners. Thank god there were some people in this town with exceptional customer care.

Within two weeks she had found an unreliable dealer called Tricky and spent half her day tracking him down via his mobile and the other half waiting for him. She was desperate and it showed and the streets are not a good place to be if you're desperate. And she knew this but she no longer cared. It was May and in the day the sun shone and the nights were warm. And the days had no beginning and the nights had no end and the weeks rolled by.

What happens when you're scoring on the street, is vile.

Vile, vʌɪl/, adjective

adjective: vile; comparative adjective: viler; superlative adjective: viles

- extremely unpleasant, "he has a vile temper"
- morally bad; wicked,"as vile a rogue as ever lived"
- *archaic,* of little worth or value, "all the feasts that thou hast shared erewhile, to mine shall be but vile"

You get the picture. The need and hopelessness are almost tangible, you can smell it, feel it, rub up against this powerful world, where the undead and mostly unwashed interact with the most ruthless of capitalists. An economy so in flux that the most expert marketing plan would not be able to keep up. All change is via word of mouth. Code either spoken or whistled rules. What was established yesterday is out of date the following day and then by evening another 'thing' has become the norm. The police push the dealers into new areas the dealers shimmy up and down roads, the runners run and the client follows being gently guided by the runners and the smell of a hit. Crack and heroin are the main contenders.

Nothing is more profitable and more prolific. The

speed and efficiency of this lucrative industry is exceptional. Its seriously impressive, no money no drugs. No favours, this is street dealing and it's ruthless. Good dealers get the good clients and it takes time to find the good ones. When you make your first street deal, you might get lucky, but usually you'll end up buying £60 worth of paracetamol. Do you really know what Heroin tastes like? So that's one in the pecking order to avoid and then it goes on and on everyday, 3 or 4 times a day or more depending on your finances.

It takes weeks and weeks of hard work and dedication to become an effective buyer of illegal street drugs. To get an established crack and heroin habit can take even longer, sometimes months of very hard graft. But dedicated is what all drug users are. And they're perseverance is impressive to say the least. Out in all weathers, putting their morals at risk, on the front line looking for good dealers.

And the dealers also face insurmountable problems to deliver their goods. The police must be seen to be doing something, so raids on crack houses are common. The local rag reports on various clean-up operations which keeps the tax paying, local home owner happy and the police make sure the house that's destined for a 6am wakeup call gets a tip off, so all the junkies can vacate. What police station wants a charge room full of incoherent bullshitters on a come down? And life goes on, round and round seeing different faces, different places, but always the same content. Supply and demand the basis or should I say bases of this economy.

Base...how low can you go?

Bally knows she's sunk to her lowest level. She does care but can't help herself and as the weeks roll on, scoring, getting high and then coming down are all there is. As spring turned into summer, an unusually hot May brings teams of bright young things on to the street and the economy grows like the flowers in Soho Square, well-watered and tended, they flourish amidst the urine soaked soil.

Bally stands in an alley way opposite a 1950's Italian Deli, the shop is packed with produce, she wonders why they bother. Her hair is dirty, her skin sallow, her clothes hang off her. Externally she's just looking slightly impatient but internally, chaos resides, all sorts of negative thoughts race across her mind, crashing into her skull, bouncing off the bone and firing off on another path. Millions of thoughts in just a few minutes, waves of thoughts the really bad ones come with bouts of nausea and stomach clenching fear.

What happens if he doesn't come?

I haven't got any money. I need him.

Jane De Croos

My body hurts, someone help me.

I've been abandoned, I'm on my own.

He's not coming, where is he?

I'm on my own, he doesn't want me.

How am I gonna score?

Her new dealer, a child called Blue (he could be no more than 15) saunters across the road towards her, smiling flirtatiously as she beams back at him. At 15 Blue knows full well what these desperate junkies will do and he makes full use of the 'job perks', keeping in mind that in his line of work there is no sick pay or pension scheme. And Bally is his ideal candidate; desperate, dirty and short of cash. And as he found out last week, when she tanks up, she doesn't give a shit. Oh and he was so ready to tank this little lady up, so so ready.

So that's how it starts, our little heroines further demise into the pit of despair. Only a short while back, she had truly believed that she was at her lowest, but as life has a habit of surprising even the most conservative members of society, she was about to sink even further.

Pete was also finding life's merry twists and turns, a touch challenging. His daughters didn't want to leave London or more to the point their friends. He had omitted to inform them of his plans to

Nearly Thirteen Months

whisk them all away on a sunshine, blue skied adventure and they weren't stupid. The eldest had allied the two younger ones and the sibling stance was 'we ain't going nowhere.' Pete was at a loss, he couldn't force them, these girls had all inherited his stubborn streak and had dug in firmly.

As he walked through Soho on the most glorious of evenings, he realised that he might have to stay. His exit strategy had been about himself, he hadn't really factored in the girls and what their lives might be like in a foreign country. London was exciting, vibrant and now in this extraordinary early summer, the inhabitants were out in full force. The city had never looked better after its long winter hibernation, the place was literally pulsating with life. He felt his cock twitch, the sun had made him horny, very horny.

And then he clocked Bally, barely registering the person who had piled into the back off him as he stopped dead in the middle of the pavement. Stepping aside to lean up against a shop front he lowered his sunglasses and watched the scene unfold in front of him. Bally had lost it, she looked done. When had he last seen her, only a few weeks ago or was it a few months? In a few days it would be June, all he knew was that in a short space of time she had lost it. Her lifeless face, dark eyes were searching anxiously. She was waiting for her dealer, he knew there would be no other reason she'd be standing there.

He didn't know why he was watching her, but felt compelled, slinking back further under the awning, he got into a place where she wouldn't spot him. The street fizzed with vitality, with life and there she was, barely standing, if you laid her out on a mortuary slab, she would have looked dead. He watched on sensing her pain, she was clucking and it was obvious, she was in a very bad place, he couldn't look away.

Five minutes passed before Blue turned up. The very young and very beautiful Blue, Pete was intrigued. Slightly tanned, approx 6ft, slim, muscular, mixed-race boy. His light-weight track suit bottoms hung off his very slim hips, whilst an even thinner t-shirt swept loosely across a perfectly formed broad chest. Pete took it all in. The boy looked like one of those sexy South American characters off the TV. But this boy was pure London, he knew the type, hard working, ruthless, dangerous and no different from the many that crossed his path. He had to give it to the kid, he had style. He watched Bally gush all over him, her smile was one of utter relief (at least she still had all her teeth). They embraced warmly, hmmmm Pete mused, she was sleeping with him, and he didn't like it. What was that feeling, that stone in the pit of his stomach, that sudden weight across his chest…jealousy? Really? Pete was taken aback;

wow he hadn't seen that one coming. Hmm-mm...suddenly London looked a different place.

Pete was an old fashioned man at heart, whom felt at his strongest when protecting a female. He'd always liked Bally, she was one of the good people. She was not malicious just misguided and he could see her struggling as she jigged desperately next to the boy, who was looking even more cool, calm and collected next to the desperate Bally. He could also see the trouble she was literally dropping into. He felt his chest tighten, he hadn't felt like this for a long time. How strange it was too feel this pull on his heart. This fucked up mess was making him reconsider his plan to get out of the UK. But Pete had always acted on instinct and his were finely tuned. He would not desert Bally, he knew that, as he stood concealed under the cover of a dirty Soho awning in Soho he made up is mind. She needed him. She needed a man. A good man. She needed Him.

Pete followed them, keeping his distance, he knew they'd be going back to her place, or where ever she was holed up. That's how it went, the women had the beds that the men dropped in to. It gave the men freedom to come and go as they pleased, and the women waited. Waited for their men to give them what they wanted; sex, affection, money, drugs. The women always waited. And this woman would be no different. She needed

Blue and right now there was no one else. Pete had seen it time and time again. Bally was hooked, hooked on the drugs and the boy that supplied the drugs, if there was no Blue there would be no drugs. She would do anything for him now and Pete doubted she had any idea what she was about to become.

The happy couple stopped at a plain white door in need of a repaint and Bally let them in, she still had her own keys, that was a good sign he thought and now he also knew where she lived. Twenty minutes later the boy reappeared on his own and set off down the narrow street. Pete watched the boy go, watched him skip up the kerb as he casually sauntered across the road without a care in the world. This kid had no idea what was about to befall him, but it was going to take time. Pete knew Bally wouldn't leave him, she was in too deep. This was going to take some planning, he was going to need some help. He made the call.

Crystal's phone flashed and buzzed at the bottom of her bag. She pulled it out and saw the contact Aunty Doris on the screen. Knowing he wouldn't leave a message she answered. She was intrigued, what the hell did he want.

"'ello stranger....what can I do for yer?" Crystal's voice was as smooth as silk, seduction hung off her every word.

Pete smiled to himself, fuck London was so sexy in the sun, he pictured Crystal's arse in her tight trousers, spanking her.

"'ello darling, as a matter of fact there is a little thing you could help me out with."

This was London no one called to ask you how you were. But manners were everything.

"Well before we get into all that, may I ask how the most beautiful girl in London is this fine afternoon?"

"Yeah, I'm enjoying the sunshine, 'n yerself?"

"What's there not to like? And I'm very well indeed, thank you for asking. Now let me get to the point, I need a favour and request a quick chat, what's a good time for you?" His direct request for a meeting didn't invite the opportunity of turning him down. Crystal was intrigued.

"I can be at Gianni's in'ner 'our?" In return she answered swiftly and professionally. They both knew neither would be late.

"That's perfect love, see yer there."

Gianni's happened to be the cafe where Pete had informed Bally that he would stop supplying her. How apt he thought, everything always connects in some way or another. Great, he had one hour to formulate a plan to help Bally. He was conscious he's just stopped himself from using the word 'save;' why was he saving this girl? Yes he wanted to save her, he felt testosterone surge through him, on a micro biological level a few hair follicles had opened on his chest. His blood was up, fuck, he felt good. This fuckwit kid was in for a rude awakening, Pete was gonna enjoy this. He would have Bally, yes, the very beautiful, ethereal Bally, would be his.

Pete thought about the objective. Get Bally to stop using drugs and then get her to fall in love with him when she's clean. Should be easy enough, haha, had he lost his mind.

Fuck why did he want this woman so much, and why hadn't he realized it before. And he wanted her, he needed her. His mind raced hmmmm, no one leaves a drug habit unless they really wanted to, that was the problem with drugs, they were very good; why would you want to give them up? But Bally was different, he was sure if he showed her another side of life, she would want it. The problem with Bally was she'd never known a life that didn't involve some sort of anesthetic. Hmmmmm he would have to get her away, he was going to need some more help.

When he walked into the cafe, Crystal got up from their usual table by the noisy coffee machine to greet him. Crystal looked good enough to eat, her hair shone in its high swishing ponytail, her teeth flashed white, framed by a sugary pink lipstick, her clothes, make up, accessories were all immaculate and her delicate perfume only added to her sense of completeness as he embraced her warmly and breathed her in, pulling away only to eye her all over again, take her all in. Fuck she looked good, and she new it. Good on her he thought. Back to business.

"Thank you for meeting me Crys at such short notice, I appreciate that you have a busy schedule and may I add you look very beautiful." Manners first, never forget your manners, he could hear his mother.

"Thank you and what can I do for you?" Crystal had done with the preliminaries.

Small talk over, Pete jumped in "Bally's in a spot of bother."

Crystal translated rapidly, 'Bally's in deep trouble' and she had a good idea what. She also clocked Pete's interest. How funny, did Pete have the hots for Bally? When the fuck had this happened?

"And how may I help you?" She was very cool and not about to get emotionally involved. Never get emotionally involved. Pete knew the routine and didn't get offended.

"Bally's not very well." He made it sound like she had a head cold, Crystal mused her friend, that she hadn't seen since that last night together, had gone the wrong way. Crystal herself had used the opportunity to knock the drugs on the head and just go cold turkey, but she hadn't been using as much as Bally and had her job to sober her up. I mean she was still drinking like a cunt, but that she believed was an acceptable and necessary transition to make, when leaving a drug habit.

When they left the air was still warm but the golden glow of Soho had turned a majestic midnight blue. They parted on good terms and embraced briefly, each with an understanding of the task at hand. Crystal laughed to herself, what the fuck had just happened, one of the savviest most expensive, most clean cut dealers in town was about to cross over to the dark side, he was about to go after a junkie, he was about to cross the line.

Everyone knew the rules 'you can't make anyone better, you can only save yourself'. Pete, Crystal believed, had temporarily lost his mind and it could only be put down to 'the power of the puss' oh dear, that was men for you. And now she too was going down a path that she wasn't entirely comfortable with. She briefly analysed her feelings and it didn't feel good. She had spent a life time trying 'not' to feel anything, a whole fuckin entire lifetime. She didn't even see her mum, but she did pay for her. Just as she'd paid for Bally's drug habit, she knew her mate was going down, she had known the girl was in a bad place and she'd walked away, she'd done nothing.

And here she was being handed an opportunity to make it all better, to make amends for all those times she's felt so guilty about leaving her mum, leaving her smashed out of her head waiting for her next john. Crystal had known as a teenager it was too late for her mum, but right now she knew it wasn't too late for Bally. Her stride became fiercer as she suddenly became flooded with a new sense of purpose. She would do her best to pull Bally back from the brink, Pete's plan was insane, but they had no other choice.

Pete walked down to the Tube slowly, he was no longer in a rush. He had no idea why he was doing what he was doing, but he knew he hadn't felt this good in a long time. He felt connected to the world; he could feel his toes, feel the material of his 100% cotton enriched socks as they gently encased his heels, his arches. The balls of his feet bounced lightly on top of the springy soles of his trainers, the hard paving slabs a million miles away. He was on his way home, he was getting back to his girls and he was gonna tell them they weren't leaving. No one was going anywhere now.

Just as Pete walked through his front door, to a variety of shouts and the sight of a slightly harassed Chloe, the girls nanny, several miles away Blue arrived back at Ballys flat and let himself in.

The dim light in the hallway only slightly masked the deprivation of the scene in front him. Her home (if you could call it that) stank. Blue wasn't on his own, he'd brought another man and this man eyed Bally. The man pulled out a handful of twenties and gave Blue five. And then Bally heard the door click shut. She was flat on her back on dirty white sheets. As she lifted her head, she felt slightly sick, but knew she wouldn't throw up. Dressed in nothing but a very tiny purple g-string, she lifted herself off the bed and leant forward on the her hands and knees and opened her mouth.

They all wanted to fuck her mouth. Her small white frame, for she was very small now and very pale turned this man on. After some clanking and rustling he knelt down with his dick firmly in his hand and shoved it in her mouth and then leant over and shoved his thumb up her arse. Arghhhh fuck it hurt, she gagged, bucked against his cock but this just egged him on. He went on to thumb her hard now, maybe he'd shoved in few more fingers she didn't know, she didn't care because at the other end she was choking. His cock now properly hard was hitting the back of her throat, she knew better than to bite down, so she just opened her mouth wider to try and let some air in. Gasp, gasp, relax and breathe and gag.

And then he pulled out and stopped, she heard him zip his cock back in his trousers; he was breathing hard. She went to sit back on her legs

Nearly Thirteen Months

and as she did so he grabbed her shoulder and pinched hard. "Do not move, unless I say so, got it!" His voice was public school and nasty, it was a command and she nodded swiftly. She wondered what this one had in store for her.

A few hours later Blue came up and they chatted. She was in love with him, he stroked her and told her over and over again, how she was his special girl and that he'd always look after her. He kissed the top of her head; he never kissed her mouth and placed a little white plastic ball and a little blue plastic ball in her hand. She looked up at him adoringly as he got up to leave once again. He was always leaving her, he had stuff to do.

She could hear the little clock tick, tock, tick, tock, every now and again she'd see the little luminous green lights of the hands as they stared back at her. Reprimanding her 'we're watching you' they would say. And when she saw them she'd turn her head away and think of nothing. The door clicked shut or had it just opened. She heard voices and lifted herself off the dirty sheets, her white fluffy duvet a thing of the past.

Nothing mattered anymore she just wanted to be high, she wanted to get the money to get high and this is what she did for it. Blue was sorting it all out for her because he loved her, she felt loved by him. It made her happy to think about them being together, if only she didn't piss him off so much, if only she could make him happy like he made her.

And the days rolled on and she began to question her sanity, she knew not what was going on and why she was being tied down, her throat was so dry she needed water. She was so grateful for sleep, she liked it better when she was asleep. Her mind whirred, thoughts raced around her barely conscious brain. Her body hurt in private places, it was so sore she could hardly stand up to get to the toilet, a strong thick yellow urine tinged with pink, arghhhh everything stung. She went back to bed cradling her little wooden box, gently tapping out a measure on to a strip of foil. Ahhhhh all was well, all was well again.

6 JUNE

I hope that you are happy

I hope that you are free

> Some Fine Day, Seamus Ruttledge

Crystal spun her hair round and tied it aggressively into a ponytail. Her temples ached, she pressed them briefly, she needed a drink. She needed the sort of drink that you woke up next day and wondered what had happened. The sort of drink you regretted, that made you shudder with shame. Her nerves were firing all over the place. Her skin felt like it was actually hurting. Exhaling slowly she pulled a Tramadol out of her purse, necked it and clipped the expensive clasp nosily shut. Cheap leather goods could never compete with that sound. It made her feel slightly irritated at the futility of all purchases. Her mind was wandering, she was nervous. Today was the day they were going to put Petes' crazed plan into action. Nearly a month had passed since their first meeting when Pete had requested her help. A lot can happen in a month. She did not feel confident, she felt committed.

She thought of her friend and how far she'd fallen. Pete had been keeping watch and was giving her regular updates; she hadn't left the flat for over 1 week now. Crystal knew Bally was beyond help. She had crossed over to the dark side, she had let go of reality and now only knew one life. Now nothing else existed apart from her drug habit. It consumed her night and her day, her wake and her sleep. There was nothing else to be done and Blue was at the centre of her demise. She was hooked on a drug which he supplied; he gave her everything she needed. She was hooked on him, she was dependent as a new born child. Arms greedily outstretched, needy flaying arms, she needed continuous care and that's what he was supplying. Every now and again he left her to cluck, left his little baby to wail and wail and wail, she was in pain and he would leave her. And when he came back she would be even more grateful for being rescued than before. He was her hero.

Slow down, Crystal told her mind, *slow down everything will be fine, just breathe.* Calming herself she realigned her mind and felt the Tramadol creep up. She felt her shoulders loosen and her pulsing temples ebb. She sat in the cafe window across the way from Bally's place fiddling with her phone with a cold cup of tea in front of her. Out the corner of her eye she registered movement and

Nearly Thirteen Months

turned without fuss, to catch Blue walking out the door. Pete had been doing his homework and Blue had turned out to be a creature of habit. Quite easily one of the biggest mistakes any up and coming criminal could make, thats if they wanted to continue with the life which they seemed to enjoy so much.

But, as we all know, life is easier when you're in a routine and Blue seemed to love his. It was 5pm and he'd no doubt dropped off some gear for Bally. Just enough to tide her over, but not enough to render her unconscious. He would be back at 7pm and he always came back alone to check all was well before the night shift. They had two hours. She would do her bit. Pete thank God had not disclosed his side of the plan and for that she was truly thankful.

By the time Crystal was out the cafe and crossing the road, Pete who had been incognito further down the road was already at Bally's door, both wore wigs, baseball caps and casual tracksuits and Pete had a big gym bag with him, they looked like they were going to/from the local sports centre (wherever that was). Pete slipped the lock expertly and suddenly they were both in. Shutting it behind them he groped for the light switch, nothing happened. Hearing the click in the darkness sent a shiver down Crystal's spine.

Turning her phone on the bright light illuminated

the filthy staircase. The walls were stained and grimy, the carpet blackened and threadbare. Neither spoke but they both felt the same thing. *How could anyone live like this?* Debris filled the hallway, flyers, post, takeaway food wrappers, rubbish, filth spilled up against the stairs, everywhere. The putrid smell sat snugly in the tight airless space. It was never a 'des res' thought Crystal, but it also wasn't fuckin' disgusting. Up they went to the flat door and Pete shuffled past Crystal to get to the lock, but the door squeaked slowly open. He squeezed Crystal's arm in comfort and they walked in.

Neither were prepared for what they saw, as they edged into the dimly lit room. They were both truly shocked. The smell was like nothing you could imagine. Filth and decay emanated off the bed, off the walls, the matted worn carpet. Pete took in the scene, the drug use, the foil, lighters etc. that was, as expected, but what was really shocking was the thing on the bed. Bally had what looked like an oversized red satin negligee on, the scene was grotesque. Both Pete and Crystal waited for their eyes to focus in the dark.

Bally lay curled over, the material of her garment lay slightly to the side of her, crumpled and dirty. She wore no underwear, her body was covered in bruises her breasts if you could call them that had bite marks all over them. She looked like a corpse from a graphic Scandinavian police drama.

Nearly Thirteen Months

Her wrists and ankles had open wounds over old bruising she was curled in a ball on a dirty bloodied sheet. Pete's foot knocked against something solid, the metal clunking sound made Bally whimper and made him glance down taking in the various chains and ropes which he presumed had been used to tie her up. His eyes got accustomed to the light he could clearly see the finger marks around her throat. There were whip marks across her thighs. Her long beautiful hair was all matted.

Crystal was moving fast, they needed to get her out. They both knew she wouldn't be going anywhere willingly so just as Bally was trying to understand what was going on, Crystal pumped a substantial cocktail of ketamine/zylazine into her arm, this would render her absolutely useless in about minutes. Pete looked at Crystal impressed, she was keeping her cool, good on her he thought. Crystal was already pulling clothes out of her bag and dressing a limp and helpless Bally. She was trying very hard not to look at the person beside her. She was trying very hard indeed, because she knew if she stopped and took stock of the condition her friend was in, she would never recover.

The bruising between her legs and the dried blood made Crystal suddenly wretch. What the fuck had happened, what animal *(animals)* had done this to her? Jesus why did she ever want to know? She hastily pulled tracksuit bottoms on a pair of lifeless legs, rolling her over like she was a rag doll, to get them over her bum, the site of Ballys bare backside made her literally gasp with horror, she was covered in what looked like burn marks from a cigarette. Crystal put her mind temporarily somewhere else and concentrated on exhaling. *Just breathe.*

Pete dropped his bag to the floor, got out a phone and started pushing buttons. Within 2 minutes Mustafa their Uber driver had pulled up 20 meters away on the corner of a pedestrian busy crossroads. The account had been set up that day with a pay as you go phone and a Mrs Carol Sanderson's debit card. She'd no doubt find out in a few days, but by then they'd all be long gone.

Pete wrapped Bally in a 'Hello Kitty' blanket he'd brought with him and carried her down the narrow staircase, Crystal was already downstairs and had opened the front door slightly to give Pete some light, they didn't speak, they didn't need to. If anyone was watching this just looked like a mum and dad putting their sleepy child into a car. Unless you were looking for something and then you just might notice the man wearing surgical gloves, but I doubt it. It was Soho on Thursday early evening and the streets were already teeming.

No one paid any attention to the family. Dad put his daughter carefully into the car and gave Crys-

Nearly Thirteen Months

tal a brief kiss on the lips. Bally was mumbling a bit but not making the fuss they thought she might, the plan was going well. Crystal jumped in next to the bundle and they drove off slowly in a rather nondescript silver Toyota Prius leaving a very 'controlled' Pete behind. Pete walked slowly back to Ballys flat and went back upstairs into the tiny little room and tapped the heavy chain on the floor with a steel toe cap. Only difference this time was he'd done it on purpose.

He began to unpack his bag and pulled out another pair of surgical gloves and put them over the ones he already had on. Then he put on what looked like an all in one thin chemical suit. Next was a plastic sheet that he'd put down on the floor, he placed it between the entrance of the room and in between the armchair and the mattress. Then for the weapon, a piece of wood, but not any piece of wood this was a piece of 2 x 2 plywood which in the right hands could kill another human being instantly. And lastly, a balaclava which he put on for a second to pull it into place, then pulled it off to leave it resting on top of his forehead.

With the balaclava in place he'd felt like an animal, a vicious predator, his blood had surged and he could feel the pump of his hammering heart. Adrenaline spiked and waned. Not yet, he thought breathing slowly as he walked into the kitchen. With his weapon in hand he swung it gently, slowly with perfect control, up and over his head and then down, swoosh, woosh. He then placed it on the counter and leaned against the sink to wait. Very faintly he heard the little clock tick, tock, it soothed and stilled him. He had begun to perspire, he could feel the heat coming off his body.

Pete could now smell the heat coming off his body. The all in one suit was warm and the balaclava perched on the top of his head didn't help either. As he leant against the wall, he thought of Bally. He thought of her broken body to match her broken mind. He wondered when he had fallen for her and why he hadn't seen it before. His rule of never getting involved with clients was one he had never broken before and he had had plenty of offers. Maybe he had just tuned out his heart to his feelings for so long now, he didn't know what it was like anymore. Love...was he in love?

He knew he would never have left her like that. He wanted to run his hands through her hair, as he remembered it all beautiful and glossy. He tried to get the picture out of his head of her lying on the bed just feet away from where he stood now. Tick, tock the little clock went, time went by very slowly, but Pete was good at waiting. Suddenly, he heard the main front door click open and slam shut, he tensed instantly.

This was it...*One chance make sure you do it proper hard,* he coached himself. He exhaled deeply, steadied his nerves, got his feet in the perfect position and as Blue came bounding around the door, Pete was ready for him. Blue didn't know what had hit him as Pete swung the piece of wood to the side and smashed it against the temple of the young boy, knocking him for six into the small room. Blood splattered up the wall, Pete and Blue had both heard it, then the room went a deathly quiet. Blue lay there very still, but alive. He murmured something in disbelief and tried to get to his feet, but could barely lift his shoulders off the floor.

Right now his brain was swelling and a hematoma was forming. Blood was pooling between the brain and the skull, trapped with nowhere to go. The more blood, the more pressure, the quicker the death. His brain was being squashed, soon he would be unconscious as the brain stopped worked properly and stopped issuing orders to the rest of the body. Finally, the organs one by one would fail and death would follow.

Pete being a man of caution wasn't taking any chances and stepping towards the boy, struck another vicious calculated blow to the kid's forehead. This was a much harder strike than the first one and connected with an impacting crunch as his skull caved in. Bits of flesh and bone and brain were flung everywhere. Pete stepped back to view his handy work, glancing down at the splatters across his chest. The boy was moments away from death, if he wasn't dead already. His body lay sprawled against the crumpled plastic sheet. His eyes wide open and staring, he looked startled not really dead, like he couldn't believe what had just happened. But it had happened, he was dead, his life snuffed out with two quick whacks to the head, all in the space of about 8 seconds.

Pete breathed heavily and pulled his balaclava up over his face. Job done. This kid was scum, he felt no remorse, he felt nothing apart from relief. The world was a much better place without the likes of him. Yes he knew he was a dealer but he didn't abuse people. His clients abused themselves, it was their choice what they did with their lives. Bally hadn't stood a chance against this smooth talking scumbag. He had hooked her to him to ensure he could manipulate and abuse her and he had. He had got what was coming to him. Pete went back down the stairs and propped a broom up against the main door. No one would be getting in even with a key.

Mustafa the Uber driver was on his way to City Airport and tried to keep his eyes on the road. Originally from Syria, he'd been in England for only five months. At twenty nine he'd seen an awful lot already and when a barely conscious human being gets carried into a car he knew it wasn't a good thing. He glanced in his mirror to see the woman in the back stroking the bundles hair, murmuring to her. Maybe they were sisters, maybe? He tried not to think. Concentrate on the road, the traffic was bad, it was London in rush hour. Nearly two hours later and after a slight change of plan to his destination, which his passenger had paid generously for upfront and directed him there herself, he pulled up in a 'pay and display' car park, which was deserted. He pulled up next to an old but in good condition Mercedes Vito which the woman had keys for and she got out and opened the side door and went back for her charge.

Crystal didn't speak to the driver until a mumbling, drunk looking Bally had been safely shoved in the back of the people carrier. The seats had been removed and she had pulled her out the car and holding her up let her stagger in via the side door. Quickly she bunched up her legs and pulled the door across. She thanked Mustafa swiftly and was very pleased to see the terror on his face. Good, he would not talk. Well, at least not to the police.

Mustafa drove off slowly and didn't look back. He was a good honest man, a dentist by trade. London was a crazy place, nothing like what he thought it would be. This was his second time being involved in something sinister, whilst he was driving. He'd been told black cabs were known as rats, they'd rat on anyone. No wonder they were losing so much trade he thought.

With Bally safely in the back Crystal flicked the central locking which made a satisfying clunk and headed east towards the Essex Coast up the A12. The traffic was bad. Pete had put a grill up between the front seats and back part, like the ones you have for dogs or goods in danger of flying about. Crystal smirked to herself, her and Pete both new what a junkie could do when she found out that she wasn't getting any more. Pete had taken precautions and she was glad. A fleeting thought crossed her mind *'I wonder what he was doing to the boy?'* She banished it quickly and looked in the mirror to see Bally rolled up sleeping soundly on the mattress they had put down for her. She was under a duvet and looked peaceful. God what the fuck had happened to her. It made Crystal's throat go dry, she gulped on a water bottle stored in the drinks holder. Pete had thought of everything...even a parched anxious throat.

Crystal pulled off the A12 onto a slip road and was heading for the coast, within 20 minutes she was winding her way down through narrow streets towards the seafront. Then suddenly right in front of her was the sign Croat Island - Tidal Causeway. She bumped the van down onto what looked like a gravel track, braked and looked out to sea. The island was a mile away and she could just make it out in the hazy distance. It was 8.30pm and the tide was out, the causeway was littered with potholes filled with the seawater. Cranking the van into first gear she edged out onto the path and set off gingerly with thoughts of salty water lapping at the tyre's. Crystal was not a strong swimmer and didn't relish the thought of being stuck on a tidal causeway with the unconscious Bally. She shuddered and kept her eyes on the island.

Once across she pulled over onto a grass verge and got out. Breathing deeply, the fresh air whooshed into her lungs. The sun was low which had turned the sky a magnificent orangey red. She had made it, relief washed over her and hoped everything was going alright Pete's end? Getting back into the van she had a quick peek in the back at Bally through the grill, her charge was waking up. Crystal started up the motor fast and headed straight on the only road towards a very large house in the distance. Pete's directions had also been meticulous, he really had thought of everything and as she picked up speed Bally had woken up and she was not happy.

As she came round a circular drive a little bit faster than she had wanted, a tall man, with a full head of wolfish grey streaked hair appeared. He came round the front of the big stately home and waved her into a garage to the side of the house. The garage doors closed quickly behind her.

'We've been expecting you." The very raffish, wolverine man growled. Crystal noticed the lack of greeting and felt immediately at ease. Bally had started banging around in the back and Crystal was more than happy to be handing her over just in time.

"Johnny will be taking you back across the island in the morning, he'll drop you off at the station at 9.15 as arranged, so we've put you in a lovey room looking out across the sea, it's one of my favourites." The slinky wolf, smiled briefly and walked her with his hand at the small of her back and guided her up a few steps to a door which lead to a narrow corridor, which he guided her down at quite a pace. Crystal was quite stunned; she had never been in the presence of quite such a commanding man. She kept her mouth shut and was happy to be led.

Up and up they went, two beautiful staircases and down another corridor. Paintings adorned the walls in heavy gold frames, spectacular tapestries hung next to them, touching duck egg blue skirting boards. The carpet a deep red was of the finest quality and Crystal felt her trainers squidge into it. Ornate chandeliers and heavy brocade curtains were everywhere. This place was amazing, she wanted to ask questions and then suddenly he stopped, signaling his intent with a small amount pressure to the left of her back as she turned in tune with this stranger. She stepped into one of the most spectacular bedrooms she'd ever been in. It looked something Marie Antoinette would have been happy to inhabit. Wow a corner room with the now darkening sky peering in from three vast windows.

Wolverine backed out of her room, assuring her that 'her companion' would be well looked after and she was not to worry. Dinner would be served in her room in 10mins and if there was anything she needed at all, she was to dial 1, and Mary would be there to help.

The door closed with a gentle click and she was left on her own. *Fuck what a pad!* Crystal slipped off her trainers and went across the enormous dark oak, four poster bed. There was a bag on the bed and she unzipped and found some clothes. Her wig was itching and she still had her baseball cap on (Pete's instructions). She was just about to lift it off and have a good scratch when she remembered dinner would be arriving shortly. Giving her hot scalp a brief massage through her hat, she went on a reccy, opening cupboards and draws of enormous bureaus, turning gold taps on yes she'd treat herself to a bath. The gold plated taps felt warm in her cold hand. The hot water gushed out, as she poured something smelly into the tub.

As she walked back into the room, there was a knock at the door and she went to open it. There in front of her stood a small stout homely woman, who was carrying what looked like the biggest tray Crystal had ever seen.

"Come on love, out the way," the woman bustled in a proper cockney accent. "Get out the door, or I'm gonna drop this." Crystal backed up in silence.

The woman was all action and good nature. She smiled briefly, hurumped the tray down and spoke efficiently. "Right now, here's your dinner love, I'm Mary give us a tinkle on 1, if you need anything. It's me lasagne tonight with a fresh salad." Crystal briefly wondered if they served any other type of salad? "Now Love, get some rest and I'll be up for the tray later on. Leave it outside the door. You don't mind me though, get yourself off to sleep and breakfast will be served at eight, on the dot. Let me know if I can get you anything else mind, just dial 1 and I'll be up in a jiffy." And with that last word she was out the door, leaving a rather stunned Crystal to take it all in.

Dinner smelt magnificent and she sloshed out a glass of decanted red wine and went to see to her bath. Ten minutes later she was submerged in the soapy, fragrant suds with her dinner plate wedged in one corner and the decanter and glass in another. She ate and drank greedily and thought about the craziness of the last few hours, as the hot water, home cooked food and alcohol soothed her mind and body. Might be best to leave her 'soul' for another time.

Whilst Crystal was escorting the very dozy Bally out of London, Pete had a body to dispose of. He went back to his bag and took out four yellow medical waste bags and a handsaw the length of a forearm, he placed the items on the mattress. There was going to be a lot of blood, his plan was to minimalise the clean up and do it in the bath. Wrapping the body in the plastic sheeting and tucking it in so as it wouldn't drip everywhere he hauled the body onto his shoulder and headed in the direction of the bathroom dumping the dead weight into the cheap plastic bath with a thump, Pete went to work with a calm and methodical approach. Stripping the boy first, he then went to remove his limbs starting with his legs at the knee and then hip, followed by elbows and shoulders. It was slow work and Pete was sweating heavily but never slowed down or faltered. Slow and steady he sawed away until he had a head (or what was left of it) and torso in one bag and various limbs in the other 2 along with the plastic sheet and Blues clothes.

The last bag he had kept solely for his stuff and he placed it aside as he began to clean up. Crystal had informed him previously of Bally's love of household bleach and when he looked in the bathroom cabinet, he had not been disappointed as he came across at least eight bottles. By the time he had finished his eyes were smarting and he could barely breathe but the place was sparkling. He placed the sealed bags in the corridor and took a final look at his handy work in the bathroom, just as Crystal was gently lowering her slender frame into the beautifully fragrant tub off the coast of Essex.

Pete pulled off his clothes and sealed them tight in the last medical waste bag. Standing naked in

Ballys room he felt strangely calm. He breathed a deep sigh of relief and got dressed in the clothes he'd brought with him. Dark jeans, dark sweater, dark trainers. It would be dark outside and he'd fit in perfectly. Finally, he pulled numerous heavy duty black bin bags out and placed the sealed medical bags in the inconspicuous black ones. One by one he carefully put them down by the front door.

Taking the lightest bag he went off to get the car. It was the one with his clothes in it, no need to be walking the streets of London with body parts. He shut the door and pocketed the key, that Blue had let himself in with. Earlier in the week he'd bought an old Saab in South London, he's already changed the plates and had parked it a few streets away in the overpriced, underground carpark. He felt physically spent but his mind was alert and keen as always. He pulled his brand new baseball cap over his eyes and slinging the bag into the front footwell he drove slowly back to Bally's flat and pulled up outside on the double yellow. Jumping out with the hazard lights flashing he quickly began to load the boot of his rather unusual cargo.

That night he would swing by Hammersmith hospital and drive round the back to where the waste was incinerated. His connection there would watch while he tossed the bags into the 1,560°F heat.

7 JULY

'Oh Faith Don't Fail Me Now,'

Faith Don't Fail, Joy Whitlock

Her mind was slow and her body heavy, her fingers felt like they didn't belong to her body, dim lighting, hushed voices, she didn't care. She didn't know where she was but she felt clean, her hair smelt of shampoo, her mouth was dry and minty, the pillow soft. She fell asleep, drifted into a long and deep place. She didn't know where she was or where she was going. She didn't care, she was gone.

Doctor Francis (the doctor part being of rather dubious origin) was a miracle worker in the field of addiction. He was a hardcore believer that people got off their nut, because they both liked it, and felt they had nothing else and that was simply that. He trained his clients in bravery, self esteem, responsibility and accountability and knew with his help if that's what they wanted, they could turn their lives around. He was also fully aware that most of his clients didn't want to be responsible or accountable. His client base was eclectic, strictly word of mouth and as you could imagine very expensive.

He had not liked the man who had contacted him regarding the girl who lay under a pink and white blanket in front of him now. The man was a professional and he respected that but something had made him slightly uneasy as they talked. "Make her well again she's very important to me" those were his words, he didn't ask how or what the treatment would entail and he didn't ask how long it would take. Doctor Francis knew he would be paid monthly and that his client would let him do his job. And he would do it very well, as he always did. For Pete was not the only professional in the South East.

The Doctor could spot the failures immediately, they all chanted the same mantra, which always started with them or he or she and never with 'I' the key word to being accountable for the way you live your life. I fucked up. FULL STOP. The full stop is very important as that was the bit Doctor Francis knew people struggled with. Once the BUT came in, you'd started to blame, hold someone else, or something else responsible and back you go round into your addiction. Oh poor, poor me! But it's not my fault, not now, not ever.

But where did it all come from, what made one

person accountable and another full of blame? The feeling of 'shame' he knew cut quick and deep. The 'shame' no one spoke of, buried itself in the centre of the soul and the wound healed into a thick gnarled scar, making it nigh on impossible to escape. Trapped in the body with nowhere to go, he knew that his patients whatever their problem, had their shame, the shame that resides, deep down inside, nestled and protected by a million and one excuses.

And how eloquent these excuses were, how beautiful and justified and honorable they were. And he'd heard them all. He looked over at his patient, he'd seen the torturous abuse her body had been repeatedly subjected too. Her body would heal he knew that, it was her mind that interested him. Could he reprogram her? Did she have the strength? He stared intently at her grey lips and freshly combed hair, she was nearly dead, just hanging in there, checking her pulse which tapped faintly, he admired her will to live. The will to survive he knew was in most, but what he wanted was the desire to change the mind. Everything could be changed in the mind, you just had to want it hard enough. The key was getting his patients to want it. To want a life.

She would be sedated for the next week to ease her gently off the hardest part of heroin withdrawal. And then slowly brought round to full consciousness, very, very slowly. Two nurses came in to pull him away from his thoughts, both women, both middle aged with grown up children and both as practical as you could find them. Doctor Francis only employed the best. They got straight to work, Doctor Francis was ready, his dictaphone clicked:

Young woman aged approximately thirty years old. Caucasian, blue eyes, brown hair, 160cm height, weight approximately 45kg. Multiple injuries to head, torso, limbs, hands and feet.

External Front: left eye socket damage, day 3 bruising, right eyebrow nicked, looks like caught on metal object, perhaps ring, from punch. Right cheek bruising, possible slapping. Lips split, sore from dehydration and being held open for prolonged period. Inside mouth tissue damage from possible finger nail scrapping on both sides. Throat bruising, looks like strangulation, various finger marks and heavier more solid bruising, possible cord tied round neck. All concurrent with approximately a week old, possibly more, difficult to tell.

Collar bone in tact, fingerprint bruising to shoulders at front, breasts, arms. Wrists heavily lacerated possibly from metal chain being left on, weight and material causing damage. Bite marks to both breasts, numerous and varying from 1 day to 1 week old bruising. Right nipple torn and infected, depicting old wound, put in 3 stitches, will heal ok, minimal scarring. Right hip bruised, pos-

Nearly Thirteen Months

sibly from kicking, as is stomach.

Ohhh ribs hmmmm Xray showing 3 fractured ribs bottom right hand side, otherwise all intact on left. Pubis bone intact, heavy bruising on inner thighs, tops of thighs looks like whip marks, repeatedly across pubis, approximately 20 or so. 2mm laceration from possible cord being tied at tops of thighs, bruising possible day old, quite fresh, wounds not healed, longest one 15cm from top of thigh to hip, 6 in total on both sides.

Bruising to both legs, old. Knees inflamed and swollen from possible extensive kneeling. Both ankles severe damage from what looks like heavy metal chain use, possible being tied up with feet near buttocks. Lacerations on both front part of feet, front and back, old wounds, infected look like whip marks.

OK ladies let's turn her over. No one gasped, just respectfully held her as gently as possible and turned her with minimal fuss.

External Back: Feet done and ankles as before, backs of knees similar bruising consistent with being tied with cord for prolonged period, bruising ranging in age 1 to 7 days, difficult to tell. Fingermarks up backs of thighs, along with burns, possible cigarette burns becoming more prolific towards buttock area. Very aggressive burning on buttock, towards anus looks like the cigarette or whatever was used was held on skin for longer and much harder. Approximately 30 burns in total covering both sides. Bite marks on back along with bruising from possible whipping. Same old same old. Head/scull no visible injury, X-ray all clear. Back of left ear lacerated, no need for stitching looks like from being pulled.

"If you could just pull her knees up and let them fall open, thank you ladies, let's have a little light."

Internal Vaginal: Heavy bruising to inside thighs on both sides, Major labia left side torn 6cm, holding 4 stitches. Major labia right side, swollen but intact. Minor labia on both sides heavy bruising and lacerations possible use of blunt metal object, grazing to vaginal walls and cervix lacerated, possibly with same blunt instrument.

Internal Anal: Repeated tearing to anus requiring 5 stitches in total 3 on left hand side 2 on top right. Heavy bruising internally from possible repetitive use with heavy blunt object, possible metal, from extent of damage.

"Ok that's it we're done, thank you ladies you've been most helpful" Doctor Francis's voice sounded thick in the small room. The women watched him walk out and got on with their job. What had just transpired had affected them all, they went about their work quietly and with care. Doctor Francis went to his office closed the door and eased himself into his chair, which creaked comfortably in his old office. He had been suitably shocked. If her body was in that state, her mind would be a hundred times worse. He prayed that she had been unconscious for most of it her assaults but somehow doubted that was the case; her assaulters he presumed had wanted her to know what was going on.

For all those who have never had to cling to the concept of 'time heals all wounds' and for all of those who have previously heard that enormously unhelpful soundbite at a time in their life when their whole existence was unravelling, coming apart at the seams, let it be said now, that dear Bally, was living each moment in sheer hell.

Her body quivered slightly, it was too tranquilized to shake, as if slightly cold, nothing more. Her face was hot, quite flushed and the drip was feeding her a 'sugar/salt' solution that would no doubt raise the eyebrow of Ronald McDonald himself. And there she lie. Alive, but dead. Dead, but alive, as her mind, body and soul set about torturing her. Every now and again she'd 'come round' and her finger tips would feel the smooth, fresh bed sheet and send a rapid message to her brain, this was real and then she'd shut down. Her body quivering just a little bit more fitfully within its sedation.

And then her mind would quiet. And when her mind was at its quietest she had a visitor. A dark and menacing visitor, who scared her. The visitor hovered silently above her bed, above her crisp white sheets. Listening to the clock tick, tick, on the wall, she waited and when she felt him swoop close to her face it made her draw in her breath with fear, gulp down oxygen in terror and then when she thought he was gone she would exhale and only then realise, she'd been holding her breath. At those moments she was grateful to be alive, she swallowed and gulped, just for a few moments and then went back to being still.

Day 2 came the following morning, as expected. And with it, long stretches of abject terror swept up against Bally leaving her exhausted, battered and bruised. She was still doped to the proverbial eyeballs but her mind was not to be stilled as it was used to. Yes the pharmaceuticals were good but there wasn't enough and reality was creeping in. The cold harsh bucket of reality was in danger of becoming the main feature. Her fear took such a hold of her she felt sure she was dying. End it all, suicide was always an option for the very brave and our Bally was oh so very brave. She clung to the sheets and gasped as another wave of fear hit her straight on, reeling she boldly braced herself for the next hit. The doctor looked on secretly, she was a fighter alright, her breath was heavy, but she didn't moan or cry out, her silence said it all. She was fighting, fighting an internal fight which he was all too familiar with. Hang in there he thought, just hang in there.

Nearly Thirteen Months

Addiction is a miserable pastime when you couldn't score. How quickly she had forgotten the good times. How quickly she had forgotten who she was, but then again had she ever known? Now she was nowhere, she only had that creeping fear, no one else...and oh my, how it engulfed her. It swept her up like the enormous swish of a giant witch's broom when she wasn't looking, leaving particles of her mind floating round the room.

She was adrift, no anchor, no life and the waves kept coming. Over and over again, minute by minute, second by second...God yes, you help me! Help me God? Fuck she'd started requesting the help of Mr Major Bullshit..there was no one else. Shit she was in real trouble. Because she thought silently, this is now real, this is me and ohhhh how that hurt. It hurt so much she couldn't breathe and then came another wave. Brrrrrrr her lips trembled and her tears slid down her face and still it came. Help me she prayed, help me and help came, she felt a small sharp prick in her arm and relax, all was well, she was ok.

Day 3 was even worse, whilst her body was heavily sedated her mind raced. The man came and talked to her briefly. She didn't care who he was, she didn't care about anything, she wanted Blue, she wanted to be back in her flat, she wanted his arms around her. She wanted to be away from where ever she was. God help me? Where are you? Who the fuck are you? I don't want this. She felt the tiny sharp prick and then things were better. God help me, not anyone else, help me....help me be with the man I love...Blue, help me, I'm on my own and I need you. She knew he'd come, he had promised her, he had told her no matter what, he would always come for her.

Doctor Francis looked down at Bally, his mind was still and at peace. He would get her through, he knew that. He touched her damp wrist and felt for her pulse, the erratic ticking indicated her internal struggle and he knew all was not well. She was alive but he was no fool, bringing this girl back to life, would make her strong enough to leave and continue her old life and he didn't want that. It was his job to get her clean but he wanted so much to ensure she would never go back to her previous persona. He wanted her to be herself, her real self, the person she had probably never been. She was lucky that she hadn't hit the pharmaceuticals that hard and had only been using heroin. At least that detox would be easier for her. He knew he could give this girl a life the problem was everyone around her.

Back in his office he pondered about the woman who brought her here and the man who was paying the bill. He had no problem whatsoever about 'dodgy', all of his clients were from dubious situations and he knew he was paid well not to question, but these two were trouble. He made a note to tread carefully. The woman with the wig was something else though. Beautiful and cold and a million miles away from human decency. His groin stirred and eyebrow raised as he smirked. Yes, what a woman and the fool of a man he was, had let her walk out the door. But what would he have done, what could he have done, asked politely for her number, possible dinner? I think not under the circumstances. What a shame he thought, as a breeze of regret rustled through him, as he went back to work.

Two days earlier (still on the Island).

Crystal woke up early and glanced round the bedroom. She had 3 hours to kill before her lift to the train station. She lay very still and thought about Bally. Wow had they really done it, I suppose yes they had. They had actually kidnapped Bally and god knows what had happened to that boy, but she knew he'd be dead or was soon to be dead. And now what? Pete had told her to go back to London and resume normal life. What the fuck? What the fuck was normal about her life. She could feel Bally around her, she could hear her friends clever voice, oh Bally was so smart, so funny, she wanted her back and was now horribly unsure how to go back to life without her. Her mind brought The Doctor, The Wolf back into the picture and she didn't know why. That day she went back to London wondering why she was leaving her friend.

Bally, many days later was thinking her own thoughts...Love, love, love, all you need is love.

Deep down in the cavity of her chest her heart heaved for her abuser, oh my days, she wanted him so much, she wanted the touch of him on her skin, the smell of him on her clothes, the sweat, the hardness of his body, the safety of his sweet talk. She could do anything if she knew where he was, I need him she thought but she wouldn't cry out. She kept it bottled in she kept it all to herself. And all the while she exhaled with caution, terrified her breath would give her away, as she heard a soft, soothing voice.

"Bally, my name is Doctor Francis, you are in my clinic, we're on an island off the South East coast. You were brought here by your friend. He wants you to get better and with my help you will. I don't want you to worry about your flat, your job or anything like that, as its all being taken care off. I want you to relax and take in the sea air as they say. If you have any questions please ask me at anytime. I'm here to help."

His accent was upper middle class and privileged. Bally looked at this very dark, almost canine man with his enormous bushy eyebrows and thin lips, his sharp handsome eyes. She looked at him, smirked and kept her mouth firmly shut. She knew it was Blue that had sorted this out and with that knowledge, she now could rest. She closed her eyes and went happily to sleep.

The Doctor looked down at this rather remarkable young woman who wasn't going to fight or ask questions. Something was wrong. She had in all respect been brought to him without consent and there she lie with an almost serene look of gratitude. The girl was at peace, she looked enchanted as if a Disney spell had been placed upon her. Time would tell he thought and glanced up at the oversized Victorian clock. It tocked heavily and he looked away, as if slightly embarrassed to be in the room with this sleeping beauty and quickly left. The girl unnerved him she was far too contained. The whole situation unnerved him, the woman who had brought her played on his mind. He'd sip a little something to calm his nerves he needed it, deserved it!

Central London several days later - 8pm

Crystal leapt off her bed to answer the all too familiar ringtone of her pay-as-you-go Nokia. The phone was so tiny she had trouble locating the answer button.

"Hello," she said breathlessly.

"Get rid of the phone and meet me on The Common in one hour." The voice was calm and commanding, it was Pete.

She was dressed and ready in 5 mins, she'd been on standby for 5 days now waiting for his call. Her nerves were shot to bits. She hadn't expected the unknown to feel like this, but suddenly she had felt connected to Bally, to Pete to all these people, to the man with the wolfish eyes. She felt anxious but didn't quite know why or what it was. She felt scared one minute and the next full of bravado. It was if she was living two different lives, the old and the new. And she didn't know what to do, or how to do it. Calm the fuck down she thought as she swung open the main doors of her apartment and strode out into the warm July evening. Time to focus, time see what she was to do next. Looking out across London she faced the dipping sun, everyone was out, everyone wanted to be somewhere.

Taxis were pouring into the city centre with their orange lights dimmed. "Beak Street, sweetheart," she sung into the open window of the black cab and within seconds she was flung back on the seat, careering towards her destination as her temporary chauffeur worked his magic, winding her through the narrow, back streets of the city.

She walked the few yards to The Common, ie Soho Square, guaranteed to be full of people, thus the ideal meeting spot if you wanted to wander and chat inconspicuously. Once again she thought about what Pete had said that they had to get on with their lives as normal. Crystal had wandered if he was being ironic.

As was to be expected they were both on time and he was waiting for her. He noticed she was looking good, but was slightly tense, but otherwise was holding up well. She strode over on her denim clad legs and wedge sandals, as if on a fashion

Nearly Thirteen Months

shoot. Wow she was a real head turner, one thing about Pete, he could always appreciate beauty. His thoughts flicked to Bally and her broken body and he banished them as Crystal leaned in to peck his cheek. But it was too late she'd seen into his soul and at that moment had read his mind. "Pete love, she'll pull through this," her voice was soft and kind. He patted her arm and they walked. He asked her how she was doing and she responded with the usual politeness and courtesy as did he. Then his tone changed and they got down to business.

"I'm getting daily updates from the Doctor, but I wanted to ask your opinion." Pete's voice was clipped and formal. Crystal was all ears.

"He says she's doing fine, he says she'll recover physically, with no lasting damage from what he can tell, but,"

Crystal shuddered slightly upon hearing the but..Pete continued.. "Cryst have you ever heard of Stockholm Syndrome?"

"Yeah I 'ave, its where the 'ostage builds a relationship wit their captor. A sort of belief that they're in it together."

"Yes that's basically it, the Doctor mentioned that Bally might be suffering from this. It was too early to tell because she was pretty 'tranqued' up at the moment but it could be something that we might have to deal with, so we need to prepare." Pete stood still and put his hands in his pocket and looked down, he suddenly looked very angry. Crystal backed up slightly attempting to put some distance between them physically.

"Pete so wot you're saying is, Bally might wanna go back to 'er flat and find the kid; find 'im?" Crystal was utterly shocked; she hadn't thought Bally would be anything other than 100% grateful for rescuing her from that animal. "Fuck Pete 'ow can we prepare, wot the fuck, wot 'ave we done?" Crystal's cool facade was slipping, she calmed herself and looked at Pete who was eyeing her. "Ok woz the plan." They were in this together and she wasn't gonna jack out now, Bally would see sense, she would see sense in the end and if she didn't they just have to make her. Pete took his hands out of his pockets and embraced her, his arms were strong and as he let her go she felt his pain. Oh he wanted Bally so much, it was ripping his heart apart. They stood their together cementing their friendship, their vow to take care of Bally, breathing in the same air. It felt good, she was empowered by him, she felt good. It had been a difficult few days, but now Crystal was back.

"What I'm planning is to get a little place in the country for Bally to recuperate in, somewhere she can relax and get back to being herself. When the time comes I'd like you to sort some stuff out for her. I'll be in touch love, take care." Crystal had no idea about Pete's three daughters. And it wasn't

Nearly Thirteen Months

exactly the choicest of times to be talking family. They parted at the gate and she set off full of intrigue about Bally's recovery and Pete's desire to take care of her. But there was something niggling at her, something wasn't quite right. She was by nature someone who trusted her instincts and the alarm bell had just gone off. Something about Pete just wasn't above board and with that she made a mental note to do a bit of digging and questioning at their next meeting. She wondered how he'd take that?

Pete hit the Tube escalators almost jogging, he wanted to be home with his girls. He wanted to tell them about the move, but not yet, patience, patience, all would be well. He held on to his faith that Bally would recover and need him, she would need him and want him and he would be there. The girls would want to be out in the countryside, the move abroad was a bit too much for them. But a move to a place where they could keep horses and invite their friends to, would be their idea of heaven. Keep the faith he thought, just keep doing what you feel is right and all would be well. He pushed the possibility of Stockholm Syndrome somewhere in his mind where he kept thoughts of his ex wife. Bye, bye he thought and shut that little alarm bell down. But as we all know that's the thing about alarm bells they keep ringing until you heed that warning. Brrring, Brrring! It rang again...But there would be no listening to the warning today, or tomorrow in fact.

Pete was struggling his body physically ached for the want of Bally. His desire to be her hero was gathering daily momentum. He fantasized about her looking up into is eyes full of admiration, adoration whilst he held her tightly. Her thin frail body moulded to his as if clinging to a life raft. He was her savior and he would never let her down. When these fantasies, which took on various formats of heroicness subsided, he felt slightly ashamed, he knew deep down at the core of his being, that it was wrong, what he was feeling was slightly off kilter but he was relishing in his dream and the cold harsh bucket of reality was being pushed further and further down for fantasies sake.

His shame niggled him as it always had done "who would want you," the voice in his head whispered..."what you? No, No, No my friend...look at you," and it reminded him of something his Father used to say in his low clipped tone, "Pete just take a long hard look at yourself, you're certainly no man," and his Father had been right, he'd been a boy of 6 or 7, just a boy.

8 AUGUST

"I don't need nobody to bleed for me! I can bleed for myself."

Joe Turner's Come & Gone, August Wilson

The weeks passed slowly with August waving a miserable goodbye to July's glorious sunshine. Day after day it poured, the greying sky swarming low and ominous. The air was chilled and damp. Bally sat at her desk, an old mahogany writing bureau in her small, but comfortable room starring out at a dark sea. It was morning and the whole day loomed ahead like an appalling job prospect. At 9pm (in 12 hours time) she would be given a Zoplicone to help her sleep. She was on 5mg of Diazapam in the morning and that was it. Her drug doses to help her get through the day were being reduced at an alarming rate.

She glanced up at the antique clock that ticked

so loudly, it seemed to bore through to her very core. Time was watching her, time was her enemy reminding her of how much she wished it away. She'd been here weeks and her body felt much recovered as she traced the scabs on her pale bruised wrist, not that she cared. She thought about Blue incessantly, without her 'little helpers' her mind raced, draining her. Exhausted from being with herself all day and night, she mentally bitched, without pause. Whoever said 'just be yourself' was a fuckin' prick! Angry and feeling very sorry for herself she knew to keep her mouth shut, Blue had taught her well. He'd say "no matter what babe, you never open your mouth, unless it's for cock of course," and he'd snigger at his own joke and she'd laugh along feeling uncomfortable at what he was saying, but she never really knew why or what to do about it.

And ooooh how she longed for him, how she wanted everything about him. She ached for his touch, his caress. It didn't matter to her what he wanted her to do for those other men, she knew it was their only way to get out and start fresh as a proper couple. He told her "just do it for us Bally, I can't do all this on my own. If you put us first you'd not doubt I'm gonna marry you, you're my girl. I want us to be together forever, just you and me, but sometimes you can be so fuckin' selfish."

She got confused as he blamed her for the predicament they were in and having no money. He accused her of liking all the men he brought to her and that she was getting turned on by them and she was just doing it to wind him up. She got confused when he blamed her for winding him up and she got confused when he said she made him like that. It was her fault he got angry, she was responsible for his bad mood, what did she expect when she made him feel like a dick.

And the list and the blame went on in her head, as she cried silently to herself. She wished she'd been more understanding and kinder and had worked harder at the 'us' like he'd wanted her to. Wished she'd put him first, like he had put her first. But oh my god how she'd tried, but somehow it was never enough. She had failed and now she was on her own, just like the times he'd get angry and leave her before, he'd leave and never tell her where he was going, or if he'd been back. It was none of her business. He'd left because, being with her, was crushing him, she was not meeting his needs, he was a man and he talked about his needs, as if he was a VIP, that she was supposed to serve at all times.

It all felt wrong, but he'd promised her and he said he was a man of his word, she knew she could trust him. He said he loved her, that he would never let her down, that he'd always love her, always be there for her. Everyday her thoughts, the voices in her head, competed for air time. Sometimes after her meetings with the Doctor she would wonder what was going on. Where was Blue, he made her question her own sanity, her own beliefs, she didn't speak to him, just listened to him tell his stories, he called them old folk tales from Czechoslovakia, where his Grandfather was from.

The Doctor told stories of goblins and witches, of children taken from their beds into their dreams and never returned to their families. One story stuck in her head of a brutal, cruel man who would drink heavily every day. He'd sit his children upon his knee and tell them stories of love and honour and bravery and the children adored their Papa, for his stories, but hated him for his cruelty to their mother. As every night he would beat their mother and they would hear her muffled screams and want to go to her but were too scared. In the morning they would see the fresh cuts and bruises shinning over the old and feel very sad. And then they would forget as he beckoned them onto his knee, to fill their heads with magical tales of far away lands and wizardry.

Every day she became more and more confused, as her meetings with the Doctor became more frequent and his stories more elaborate. One day, after many weeks in silence, which the Doctor didn't seem to mind whatsoever, she spoke up. Her voice surprised her, it was hoarse and little in comparison to the Doctors melodic, deep enriched tones. When had she last spoken?

"He loves me," she croaked, leaning forward to gulp water, her throat was not working properly, well not as it used to.

The Doctor continued to gaze out to sea from his office window as he always did and leaned back in his old chair which creaked comfortingly and replied.

"Who loves you?" His voice was soft and inviting.

"He loves me, the man who is taking care of all this!" She boomed! Her voice had grown in strength and with that, so had she. She flung her arms up to encompass the whole house.

The Doctor was prepared and continued to stare out to sea, breathing in deeply as the tide crashed against the shore, his eyes closing.

"Ahhhh what it is to be loved, cherished, adored." And sighed a sorry sigh as he began another one of his tales of spells, mythical creatures and sorcery. Bally sat back in the overstuffed, oversized armchair and closed her eyes, her revelation had thoroughly drained her.

This time the story was about a young girl who went to the underworld through a small hole in the trunk of an old oak tree, deep in an ancient forest. In the underworld she sat with the Devil himself and he gave her sweet hot chocolate to drink and let her look through his magic glass at all the tricks he was playing on the living. She laughed at the stupidity, of these humans and did not think for one moment that she was one herself. The Devil held her close and fed her sweets from an antelope's skull. His long fingers wrapped around her head, stroking her beautiful long red hair. When he did this she wept with joy as she missed being stroked and touched so much. Her Mother and Father had died of the fever when she was born and now she was looked after by an aging aunt. The aunt never touched her to caress her or stroke her face to soothe her and oh how she craved that simplest form of human contact. She longed for the feel of fingers upon her skin, her back her arms. She dreamt about it and wished for it and on her twelfth birthday her wish had come true. For that's when the old oak opened up to her and led her down into the underworld.

Bally hadn't realised she had dozed off and stirred as the Doctor creaked out of his chair. She could hear the sea, it was mesmerising. She wanted to hear the rest of the story, what had she missed? She had never been interested in any of the Doctor's stories before. And asked as he went towards the door to signal that their session was over.

"Wh what happ en ed… to the girl?" She stuttered, her vocal cords once again letting her down.

"Who knows Bally, who knows what happened to her, what happens to any of us?" And with that closed the door gently, but firmly behind her.

A bit too quick for Bally's liking as she suddenly found herself all alone in the beautifully polished oak paneled corridor. Her loneliness felt so deep rooted it actually hurt and she swayed slightly in unison with the tide she could not see and leant on the cool wood for support. Touching the beautiful panelling she wondered if it would open up for her and take her into the underworld. Right now she wouldn't mind being stroked by the Devil and with that she walked a slow and tiring trudge to her room. It was nearly dinner time and she always ate in her room. She sat heavily at her desk and placed her head in her hands. *What the fuck am I doing she thought, what the fuck is happening to me, who am I. I don't want to be here.*

After what seemed like an eternity Mrs Pots, as Bally had nicknamed her, came bustling in after a quick rap on the door. The food smelt delicious, she can't remember when she had ever been this hungry, but put it down to a) Mrs Pots incredible culinary talents, b) not doing any drugs, c) not having anything else to do. Mrs Pots, probably the cheeriest person alive, was full of gossip regarding the household affairs. Bally invariably tuned her out but today she looked up and smiled at her. Mrs Pots smiled affectionately back, plonked the tray down and went on to describe the meal in detail.

"Oh it's me chicken pie today, I know it's one of

your favourites and the pastry I rolled it out this morning. I know how much you love me puff." Bally stifled a giggle. Mrs Pots was not to be deterred.

"It's getting chilly out there now and I've told 'im (the gardener) he'd better be getting those apples down 'fore a storm does, well I can remember what 'appened last year when he couldn't be bothered. And nowts changed this year as he's carrying on with another lady friend. He's too busy weeding her bushy garden than his own!" And with that she bustled out of the room, leaving Bally to chuckle to herself and attack a delicious dinner which she ate with relish.

As she was eating she noticed the little silver teapot on the tray accompanied by a delicate china cup and saucer. She always had water with her meals and wondered what was in it. Peering in she wafted the most delicious chocolate aroma she had ever smelt. It literally warmed her all over, she pushed her plate to the side and poured a cup through what she believed to be the most perfect pour from a spout she had ever come across. Not one drop stained the white linen napkin. Holding the tiny little cup to her lips with both hands she sniffed the beautifully glossy rich liquid and then sipped. Oh my days, she was in heaven (ahhh nothing this good could come from hell and briefly wondered what had happened to the young girl in the story once again). The taste of this drink was like magic itself, it was so smooth and just the right amount of sweetness and thickness and cream...hmmmmm delicious she thought and continued to sip away, leaning back in her chair and closing her eyes slightly. Ahhhh this must be what it means to relax, that is relax without the use of drugs or alcohol. Who knew eh? And smiled a happy smile to herself.

Earlier, Mrs Pots had crushed a muscle relaxant in the best tasting hot chocolate in the whole wide world and Bally took to her bed soon after dinner and lay there relaxed and happy with the world, falling into a deep sleep missing her night time Zopiclone dose. The Doctor was going to rather cleverly trick Ballys mind into thinking she could do without her sleeping tablets, he was going to very subtly break her drug dependence, by making her believe she no longer needed such help to go to sleep. The muscle relaxant would be disguised over the days in various foods/drinks, but would always be associated with something very calming and pleasant. She was waking up consciously and once off the drugs he would up the work on her dependency to her abuser. He had already started by planting the seeds of doubt within his folk tales. Slowly, slowly he reminded himself, this one was going to take time.

The Doctor sat in his office and mulled over Bally's first sentence *'he loves me' 'he loves me' 'he loves me' 'he loves me.'* What she had said had given him enough ammunition to work on changing her belief system. *'He loves me'* she had not said 'I love him' but *'he loves me.'* He knew now from those three words that no one had ever put her first, no one not even her parents had ever done anything to make her feel that she was loved. Bally needed someone to love her, no wonder it was so easy for her abuser to mistreat her. Bally emotionally had been left wide open, by what he presumed was her parents neglect, wide open for more abuse, just in a different format this time. All Bally knew and understood was that when someone loved you they sometimes did things that you didn't like, but that was OK because they loved you. His chest heaved at the childhood this child must have suffered and went back to his notes. The more she would talk the more he would understand how to treat her. All he had to do was get her to talk.

And he knew she would talk he always knew she would talk, it was human nature to want to communicate. As it was to want to be stroked and held, Bally also wanted to be loved and cherished, just as the girl in the story. And in responding to that particular story she had revealed her inner most fears. All the Doctor had to do was keep telling different stories and wait for the one to impact her the most. It had worked and the hot chocolate would keep it in her memory, she was now, he believed linked to the story and that he believed to be a great starting point in her recovery.

And so the Doctor planned their next meeting and the story he would tell her, he worked late into the night, creaking in his old leather chair, musing over what it is to be loved and to love in return. The winds howled round the big old house that night as the Doctor slept. He dreamt of the woman in the wig, the one who had brought the girl. He dreamt of her body up against his, the soft smoothness of her skin, the smell of her. When the morning came he felt a touch of sadness cross his heart and ran his hand over his chest to quell the ache. Would he ever see her again? And he wasn't the only one, as on the other side of the house, his patient was once again struggling with her own demons.

Bally had woken early and she was frightened, she had dreamt of the door splitting in two and a snarling monster behind it. She knew it was just a dream and steadied herself but, she was scared and daren't turn to look at the door. She lay there curled in a ball with the duvet covering her head, too scared to move, her heart thumped erratically in her chest, knocking against her ribcage. She exhaled loudly and forced herself to turn round. The door as expected was intact and there was no monster behind it. Sitting up she thought how foolish she was and was slightly annoyed if not angry with herself, for giving in to such childish fears. But even as her heart rate slowed she noted she was still scared and stayed in bed for a bit longer than usual, cuddling up against the glorious goose down quilts.

Today she was planning to go for a walk with one of the other patients, the Doctor had introduced them by bringing the woman to her room a few days earlier. The other patient had an eating disorder, she was anorexic and looked like a skeleton. The woman knew she looked awful and pulled at her clothes, as Bally eyed her suspiciously. Thus, their first meeting had been awkward to say the least. Their second was scheduled for 8am before breakfast and Bally prayed it would be easier as she was looking forward to walking down to the beach. She would get rid of what she presumed was her chaperone and take in the sea air in solitude.

The clothes that had been supplied fitted well and were good quality. Everything was good quality in the house, as she tugged the aran wool jumper over her head and slid into thick corduroy, high waisted trousers. Definitely a bit dated, but as she gave herself the once over in the thin mirror on the back of her door, she was pleased with how she looked. In however long it was, weeks now, she had no recollection of how long she'd been on the island, she had put on weight and looked slim instead of emaciated. She'd had her hair cut to her shoulders, by the all talented Mrs Pots and it shone and she swished it around her neck. She liked the idea of looking better than Miss Nervosa, it made her feel good to think she wasn't fucked up like her. Slipping on her sheepskin slippers she walked with a new vigour out of the door and down the long paneled corridor to the kitchen. Personally she wouldn't pick the kitchen as the rendezvous spot for an anorexic, but hey, that wasn't her problem.

Ann was struggling in the kitchen, the smell of bacon was eating at her insides, she was literally weakened by her need to devour, satiate her cravings, swallow, digest. She hung onto the fiercely scrubbed work surface and prayed for her companion to be on time. Today she had agreed to go for a walk with the girl who thought she was too cool for school and would eat breakfast with her. The Doctor told her in a cheery tone that breakfast was the only meal one had to eat, the rest were a waste of time and chuckled at his own wit and left her wondering what on earth this man's credentials were. She had been in and out of psychiatric units all her life, as she'd worked tremendously hard to starve herself to death. Her elderly parents had almost given up and this, she believed was their last attempt to turn her into one of the living. Thank god she thought breezily, after this shocking waste of time and money, I'll be able to starve myself to death and be left alone to joyously count every calorie and fatty ounce. Anyway, she had a plan, she would humour the Mad Doctor and eat a small breakfast then throw most of it up and then burn the rest of the calories that remained during the day. She knew it all.

With this in mind she straightened up and eased herself off the bench top's, white knuckle ride she'd got on earlier. And whilst she was collecting herself into a stance that supposedly mimicked a normal person, Bally padded softly into the kitchen. They caught each other's eye and nodded/ murmured a sort of ineffectual greeting. Bally pulled on her wellies as Ann opened the door with a crash and finally after a bit of a todo they were out in the open air, heading towards the beach. Two women desperately trying to escape each other and the embarrassment of being forced together.

Ann, at 35 was only few years older than Bally, but looked in comparison drawn and feeble. She glanced over at Bally's rude health and wondered what the young and very beautiful girl was doing in the care of the Mad Doctor. Bally could feel her glare as they walked steadily in silence. Not discussing where they were going or what they were going to do. It appeared each had an agenda, which the other was not privy to. Bally walked slowly in front down the narrow path, allowing time for her companion to keep pace. Bally wondered if this woman would make it to the beach, let alone back again. She fantasized about her dropping down dead of a heart attack and standing over her cold body as the waves lapped against her head, she would be a hero and save her.

"Ahem" she felt a prod in her back...," I was talking to you," said the voice. It was a sweet, rather mischievous voice with a gentle Liverpool lilt. Bally turned, but kept walking.

"Sorry I didn't hear you," her voice came out, as it should and she was relieved in a self conscious way."

"I suppose if the Mad Doc has got you 'tranqued' up, I'll forgive you," the response was light humoured.

Bally replied easily "Unfortunately not," Haha...Mad Doc! That made her chuckle, he was totally nuts!

They walked on slowly in silence, the initial conversation forgotten and went down to the water's edge. It was a beautiful morning, the sun was rising and the small beach was deserted. The air was fresh and cool. They both breathed in deeply, staring out to sea.

"Whats your name?" Bally surprised herself by hearing her own voice. It had been ages since she'd talked to anyone.

"Ann and you are?"

"Bally, as in dancer," and she briefly remembered Pete calling her that. It seemed like another life time ago. What was he doing now. He was funny… but more importantly she could do with scoring off him.

Ann watched the girl's face go blank as she went off to a place in her mind, a distant memory or dream. She brought her back.

"That's a bit of a weird name, but it does sort of suit you, you're very poised."

"Thank you, that's kind of you to say," and Bally meant it, she rarely got compliments and when she did she brushed them off and then suddenly this corpse was saying nice things to her and she found herself enjoying the praise.

"I mean, you got lucky, cause imagine if you'd been called Reed and turned out to be a fat lump?" Haha they both smiled.

"Or Lucky," Bally quipped and got run over?" But the earlier joke was now flat. And they turned away shy of their previous enthusiasm to engage.

Ann suggested they walked further along the beach and then back to the house across the dunes. She was already exhausted.

"Yeah sure," Bally replied gently. "I'm knackered," she politely omitted the 'and also ravenously hungry' part. "Sea air eh!" *Errrrr and lets not mention you're starving to death.*

Ann walked slowly taking the lead. The sand made it heavy going across the dunes and she stopped several times to catch her breath, whilst Bally waited patiently. The last time she stopped with the house in sight Bally gently patted her back and murmured, "Take it easy, we've got all day," and with that Ann pushed on slightly irritated by her own lack of stamina and the touch of another. Bally had felt her companion freeze underneath her hand, her cold bony spine leaving an unpleasant memory on her palm and made a mental note not to touch her again. Ann had noted Bally's repulsion upon touching her. It was how it always had been she knew she was repulsive.

The unusual companions went round the side of the house to the kitchen door and were greeted by the warmth of the Aga and the mouth-watering smell of fried pig. The place was deserted, but breakfast had been left out. Ann sat at the table immediately, Bally noted, obviously to prove a point. Bally joined her after getting into her sheepskin slippers, which she was now realised she was in love with, which put a smile on her face. The old stove cranked encouragingly as they lifted large silver domes to reveal plates stacked high with bacon, eggs and buttery muffins.

The girls helped themselves. Bally ate like a horse, Ann like a bird, a very small bird. Peck, peck she went, snort, snort went Bally, any moment now she might start whinnying. But they ate, they both ate and they ate in silence.

There was no clock in the kitchen and time stood still for one precious moment. It graced both of them like the hand of God sweeping across the skies to change the weather in a bygone Biblical era. They both knew something had changed and they were alone and together all at the same moment. Time had passed and they looked at each other and felt lost. Bally felt like crying, but didn't. Ann looked at her and felt something she didn't know how to describe it, she could see the tears well in the young woman's eyes. All she could do was place her hand on hers. She kept her hand there. Bally felt the cold touch and was warmed by it, oh how she wanted more and with that she bit back the tears and looked even further away as her mind raced.

Touch, just one touch from another human being, she was desperate, she needed Blue so badly. She wanted him to just be there like he had been before. The way he would swagger in and sometimes smile at her if he was pleased. Sometimes he would sit next to her on the bed and stroke her hair. But she was careful not to embrace him or touch him back, because he didn't like that, he said he didn't feel comfortable after knowing what she'd been touching. He said she was dirty, a dirty little whore. She couldn't defend herself, he was right. Her mum had said the same thing that she was dirty and needed cleaning. And then she'd clean her and it would hurt and Bally would cry to herself and thank her Mammy for making her bright and shiny again.

The days rolled on and Bally met Ann every morning. They would walk slowly in the rain, it seemed to rain endlessly. Then they would meet in the afternoons and play cards, Ann taught Bally to play Rummy they were both rubbish. Neither cared to win or lose, they talked intermittently. Ann was quite taken with Bally, she had never met anyone like her before. She enjoyed her wit and bizarre sense of humour and wondered what had brought her here as the girl obviously didn't have an eating disorder or any mental health problems, she hadn't enjoyed another human being like this for a long time. Bally was funny, she was good fun to be around.

One morning as they both walked side by side across the flat sand to where the sea lapped up against the shingle beach Ann asked her.

"Why are you here?" Bally slowed slightly but didn't falter, her voice was clear and precise as she turned to address her companion.

"I'm not, I'm a figment of your imagination...unfortunately you've lost your mind!"

With that Ann stopped dead pulling Bally abruptly by the arm to face her. Bally could see the panic in her eyes!

"What? What did you just say?" Ann had been questioning her sanity for some time now as she had been having both auditory and visual hallucinations. Her voice had a harshness to it that made Bally instantly regret her silly joke.

"Whoa slow down I was frickin' joking, what the fuck, I'm really sorry, I didn't mean to freak you out." Ann was now sobbing with her face in her hands, just as the rain began to lash down. "Shit mate I'm really sorry, it was just a joke, a stupid joke."

Bally went over to her and held her tight, fuck she was tiny. Ann continued to sob. Big heaving sobs like a child.

"Ok hun lets go back and get dry," Bally whispered after five minutes had passed. Leading Ann slowly back to the house, with the rain whipping against them, they were both drenched, but neither seemed to care as they trudged up to the back door. As always breakfast had been left out for them and no one was around. Bally helped Ann out of her wet coat and sat her on the bench to pull off her boots and tuck her revolting bony feet into her own sheepskin slippers, the woman really was skeletal. Shrugging off her own coat, she sat Ann in the rocker by the Aga and poured her a tea putting a heap of sugar in it.

Ann looked very ill, her face was completely

ashen and her earlier slightly pink tinge had disappeared. Bally had noted Ann's slightly flushed cheeks on their walk and had hoped her friend had stopped purging and was on the mend. But looking at her now, she was wondering whether she had suffered some kind of stroke. Her jaw was slack and her eyes dead, she was in shock, Bally new that and made the decision to wait for ten minutes to see if she'd recover, before raising the alarm. Ann sipped the sweet, strong tea closed her eyes, rested her head back on the rocker and let out an enormous sigh. A few moments passed before she whispered. "I don't know what I'm doing, I don't know what the point is, I don't know what the point is. I am nothing, I, I, I'm so fucking tired, I'm so fucking tired of being alive."

Bally sat very still on a chair pulled up to the Aga opposite her. She sipped her tea and kept her head down. The silence in the room engulfed them as the wind howled against the back door, screaming to be let in. Bally breathed in unison with the storm, it calmed her and she quite forgot her companion and couldn't have told you how long they sat for, until she heard Ann speak again.

"I want to kill myself, I want to die of starvation, I want to have nothing inside of me I want to feel as empty as I know I am. I've always wanted to die this way." Her voice was raspy and hollow.

Bally kept her head down and spoke without

thinking.

"Didn't they have a Careers Advisor at your school?" And as soon as the words came out, she was laughing, her sipped tea sprayed across the floor, her face all scrunched up. She couldn't stop. Ann looked at her incredulously, and began to giggle, she didn't know what was funny, but it was stupid the whole thing was stupid, life was fucking stupid and that was funny. And the girls, these new friends laughed and they blew their noses and wiped their tears on the tea towels over the Aga door and that made them laugh even more.

The Doctor watched the proceedings on a camera from the comfort of his office, their laughing was infectious and he smiled with them, personally congratulating himself on the progress both women were making. Slowly, slowly he would treat his patients. He would not encourage them to live life differently or talk about self-esteem and how to raise it. His treatment was based on understanding his patient's quirky mental states. He would give them a safe place to begin to understand their view of the world. His patients in time would begin to feel that it was ok to explore their rather unorthodox belief systems. That it was interesting to think differently, his patients knew they would not be judged or manipulated into change, that if they wanted to stay the same way they were welcome to. The Doctor was giving them a lifeline from their own suicides, they knew it and most were truly grateful.

9 SEPTEMBER

Indian summer

noun

> 1a period of unusually dry, warm weather occurring in late autumn.
> ◦ a period of happiness or success occurring late in life.

Pete sat at the breakfast table with his kids, he'd called a meeting and the younger ones were making various complaining noises and pulling stupid faces. His eldest, who was far too mature for face pulling, protested via a spectacular chair scrape from one side of the kitchen, around the table, to the empty space by the door. The whole scene could have easily rivalled a Torville & Dean finale. When his darling daughter was finally seated the room fell silent and six inquisitive eyes stared deep into his. It was unnerving to say the least. He cleared his throat and began.

"I know you don't want to go abroad and I realise

that I didn't take your needs into consideration when I came up with that plan. I apologise." Silence, his offspring had learnt how to conduct themselves from the best. He continued...

"I need to tell you what's going on. *(pause)* Things are difficult in London at the moment and we need to move in the next month. I propose we don't go too far and go to the countryside, a bit outside London." More silence.

"It would mean changing schools, but your friends could come and visit us in our big house in the countryside." More silence. *(fuck it, he had said 'countryside' twice, stop frickin' selling it so hard).*

"We won't be more than an hour outside London." Nothing, the silence ensued.

He could also play the game.

"If you would like to say anything about the move now's your chance." His tone was relaxed and nonchalant, he hoped?

Juniper his eldest had been watching her Dad and knew when he was like this he meant it. She could either go along with him or her life would be very difficult. She decided to meet him half way. And anyway she'd had enough of her best friend Kelly for ages now. She was being a complete bitch. She spoke without hesitation.

"Yes dad, going abroad was not for us and thanks

for saying sorry. I like the idea of moving to the countryside, we could all have a pony." Her voice was strong and sensible.

"I want a pony." Little Gracie squealed.

He looked at Pearl his middle child and raised an eyebrow.

"Yep I'm in," she said excitedly. "Whats the house like, have you got pictures, are we going to have cows, I want a chicken?

"Chickens shit everywhere."

"Juno why are you being a cow?" Gracie yelled.

"Yay at least we don't need to buy a cow now," Pearl was definitely the one with the wit!

Suddenly the questions came fast and furious. Pete smiled a broad, parental smile, his kids enthusiasm was infectious. He loved them all so much and his thoughts drifted to Bally, he hoped, very much, she would be up for this. He would do his best, that's all he could do.

Talk of the countryside went on all day and finally with his girls in bed and the babysitter glued to some utter tripe on Netflix, Pete was out the door on his way to meet someone he probably shouldn't.

On the other side of town Crystal was in her flat

pondering life. Bally's situation had shone a different sort of light on to her own lifestyle choices. The last time she'd gotten 'on it' with her mate, she had vowed never to drink or take drugs again. She remembers them both doing it. "That's it for us, it's all clean living from here on now!" Laughing together at the productivity of it all, no doubt both believing in their mantras, "Work hard, get rich, be accountable." It had all been so righteous, so easy, as they inhaled their way through the crumbly, yellow rocks.

Crystal replayed the moment on that last night together, when looking over at Bally she had seen her mother. Her mother's tired old haggard face staring back at her. The vision had lasted a split second and had understandably shocked her to the core. It had made her do a double take and she had been visibly shaken. Bally thankfully was so twatted she hadn't even noticed. She wouldn't have wanted to have to explain that one. She knew then if she didn't stop this would be her in ten years. In that split second in time, she had received a very direct warning from the universe and fuck, she had listened. She sipped her tea and looked up to thank God. Thanked the God that had given her a snapshot of her future, the God she had never before believed existed and then she cried.

She cried for all those years she had never cried. All the times she had wanted to cry and had bitten her lip to stifle her emotions, all the times she had wanted to open the flood gates and had held them firmly in place, with a slow exhale of her calculated breath. Now all of a sudden, she allowed herself to let go, she was scared for her young life, scared of her drug taking, scared for her mum, when she'd been little. She was vulnerable, she had been so vulnerable, just a little girl. She said it out loud which made her laugh "I am vulnerable," "My name is Caroline and I am vulnerable," the words came so easily, it was as if something had unlocked inside of her and flown away.

Crystal had died that very moment and boy was she happy to say 'goodbye'. Laying down she closed her eyes and prayed that she would be OK, she prayed that she would survive the long days and torturous nights ahead. She prayed to her God, the God that had never forsaken her.

For Caroline, the street drugs and alcohol had been relatively easy to give up. If she was honest with herself, she had had enough of them. The problem and she was realising slowly, how big of a problem the pharmaceuticals were, the prescription drugs, the ones that do what they say on the tin. She'd had no idea how dependent she could become on the little pills. Of course she knew she was hooked, she just hadn't known how hooked. She had had no idea how long it would take to feel normal again. She estimated about 3 months. Ouch her head hurt just thinking about it.

Nearly Thirteen Months

She had been woefully unprepared and hated herself for being such an amateur. She had had to ween herself of slowly. It had been months and she was still taking half a Zopiclone to sleep and 2mg of Diazapam 3 times a day. The rest of the time she was white knuckling it and felt like shite. On the odd occasion she had fallen off the wagon, but on the whole she was sticking to her reduction plan and working through the headaches, anxiety, sheer terror, sweats, nausea.

Going cold turkey from heroin lasted about 3 days. Your body ached to the point that it would be easier to die. Each super sensitive hair follicle twitched nervously as your skin grated to the sensation of being alive. Every split second was a roller coaster of emotional and physical pain, made even more agonising by the simple fact that one big fat pea sized lump of brown, for a tenner, would take it all away. In comparison her pharmaceutical addiction made heroin withdrawal look like a walk in the park, on a very nice day.

Her nipples were so hard and cold at one point during the early days of her withdrawal, she had heated up hand towels in the microwave and shoved them on to her chest, in an attempt to thaw them out. It hadn't worked, her frozen skin was so sensitive that she daren't undress. Her mind so scrambled that on one very bright afternoon, she had to abandon her shopping basket at her local Tesco Express and make a dash for the safety of her living room floor, where she clung to the fluffy rug out sheer of terror. A fear she had never known before, the fear of what might happen next. She was terrified, but she didn't drink, didn't guzzle tablets and certainly didn't smoke. She had trained her mind over many years, her modus operandi was show no weakness. In other words shut the fuck up whining!

Being merciless in the treatment of her own emotional and physical state, was what was keeping her together and she knew it.

Yes she'd done the drugs and drink like her friend, but there had always been something else in her life she wanted more. Caroline wanted to be someone. She wanted to be famous, and she let the fantasy run riot most days. She fed this fantasy, she grew it from infancy, when she shut herself off in her room away from her mother talking shite and some John or boyfriend or pimp making himself the centre of their fucked up moronic world. She had then gone into her glorious bubble, it was beautiful there. It was sexy and people wanted her, people adored her, people admired her. She was desired. She was number one, she was famous. She wasn't in her right mind, when the voice of reason requested she get a grip and thus was able to carry on blotting out the reality at an alarming rate. It was easy when you made money you could even fool yourself.

Nearly Thirteen Months

Caroline went to work. Her work is what saved her, she felt in control in her rented office, where she was the only member of staff. At work she was safe and she worked hard at keeping it that way. She returned emails and calls. She was in demand, companies wanted her to present her motivational talk. Her rough working class, no nonsense accent was a bonus. She had come from nothing and made it, she was living proof of her own marketing. What a pile of shite she thought, she wasn't even interested in the money any more. She didn't know what she wanted, but she knew she didn't want to continue to con people and make them feel what they were, wasn't good enough. Capitalist fucking bullshite. She was suddenly aware of how tired of her life she had become, tired and bored it was all so pointless. Who the fuck was she anyway? Did anyone ever know? She pushed her thoughts aside and knuckled down. Work would set her free.

That same morning Pete stepped his way across Hampstead Heath, he had trainers on and was enjoying the slight incline of the path he'd just joined. September had been very dry, after the worse August on record and the Heath was lush and green for it. Birds were singing, the sun was shining, it was warm about 18 degrees and Pete with swim kit slung over an immaculate grey t-shirt, looked very gay. The male only swimming pond usually adorned with 'wanna-be' Abercrombie & Fitch models was quiet and private in the week. The perfect place to meet his man. In fairness to Pete, he had tried to give up his enterprising and lucrative business, but he enjoyed the deal too much. He enjoyed being part of the criminal underworld and felt he was good at it. A place where he was respected and in control.

By nature Pete was an introvert, not the shy type, more the type that just wasn't interested in any part of society. He was no team player, never participated for 'the fun of it' and only ever worked at his own interests. He was also an expert at self-deception. He was so good at it he had no idea he was even deceiving himself, in fact he truly believed to be in touch with his core and spent many hours contemplating how much more in tune he was with his mind, body and soul in comparison to others. When in comparison mode, his thoughts tended to lead to Bally and went roughly in this direction;

1. I will show her how to live life to the fullest
2. She will understand the person I am
3. She will be in awe of me
4. She will be eternally grateful for saving her
5. She will think I'm amazing

6. Together we will be amazing

Heading for the lockers he stripped off to his dark blue swim trunks, secured his bag in one locker and his phone, wallet and keys in another. He'd already clocked his man and with the ease of someone out window shopping strolled to the pond edge and dove in. Arghhhh it was freezing. His supplier was a twenty something Macedonian called Jovan. They raced lengths together for at least ten minutes until the younger man pulled up to the decking, treading water in the murky pond, breathing hard.

"Easy my friend, you old man, I kill you." Jovan's English had improved since they're first meeting nearly three years ago.

"Really?" Pete laughed in response, his breathing already back to normal.

Jovan had the body of a street fighter, tight, wiry and crisscrossed with scars and tattoos. The physique of someone who had no doubt fought his way up the criminal ladder maiming, stealing, probably killing where necessary. He ran a tight and effective supply chain and Pete trusted him, well, trusted him as much as you could, with someone that wouldn't have a problem slitting your throat.

"And you family, they are health?" Jovan was still catching his breath. His green eyes sparkled, his smile was beautiful, he was a very attractive man,

Pete wondered if he was gay.

"Yes mate and yours? Noticing several other swimmers eyeing up his supplier. Jovan had a masculinity and feminity about him that was very unusual in a hetrosexual man.

"Yes my friend, with Gods looking my beautiful wife and children are well." And with that he placed his palm on his chest and then slung his arm across Pete's shoulder. "Come, we swim." They both pushed off and swam out slowly to the middle of the pond, talking money and drugs as they went.

The September sun shone above them as they swapped locker keys, joked, chatted and went on their way. Pete took a different route, it was one thing carrying tens of thousands in used notes, but a serious infringement in UK law to be walking about with kilos of heroin and cocaine. He needed to be off the street fast and made his way just a few roads down, where he'd parked his car. From there he'd drive to HQ, an old warehouse on Station Road in Tufnell Park, a few minutes away. This is where he'd cut the heroin with paracetamol, it was far too strong. The coke would be bagged into eight balls or turned into crack. His crack was expertly made and his clients paid for the best. His profits would be enormous, his business model was a marketing and financial advisors dream. He worked alone, he loved this aspect of the job.

Nearly Thirteen Months

He never touched the powders or paste, he liked the methodology. All cooks had their recipes and methods. Pete had refined his over many years.

Cooking Crack – Method

1. Add a whole load of cocaine to a saucepan
2. Add water (not too much, just enough to form a runny paste), heat gently and stir to break down all the lumps.
3. Now add baking soda (not too much) keep heating gently and stir.
4. Now keep moving the pan, swirling, keep swirling
5. Add more water, slowly, slowly.
6. Wait for it to start bubbling, gently gently, not too much heat, keep swirling.
7. Wait for it...keep swirling the pan.
8. Wait for it...keep swirling the pan.
9. As soon as its stopped bubbling, stop swirling immediately.
10. Now rinse in cool water.

Jane De Croos

Ta da! What you should be left with is a crusted layer of freebase cocaine. What you'd probably get, if this was your first, second or tenth attempt is a pile of shit. Pete was an expert, his crack was beautiful. He'd perfected his method over many many months, he'd worked hard at understanding the chemical reaction, the precipitation that would take the solution to a solid. He could do it by eye just as any top chef could whip up a soufflé and produce it from an oven knowing it would never collapse.

He didn't over cut his heroin either, just enough dilute to ensure his clients wouldn't drop dead. He always measured the same, continuity of product was a large aspect of the success of his trade. He'd learnt that one from McDonalds.

So he spent the afternoon chopping and stirring. And by early evening he was finished and had sorted packages into individual consignments with a street value of approximately £20k, which he would distribute that evening, making roughly 60% on the heroin and 45% on the crack and cocaine. That's a lot of cash. Yes he could make more, but he wasn't greedy and he was always safe. Well as safe as you could be when you ran drugs all over the centre of London. On some nights he could make up to £30K, Christmas was always busy.

He met his clients in cafes, bars, restaurants and

Nearly Thirteen Months

work. He never sold to impulse buyers (the ones who just fancied a hit after a drink), never went to a home address and never dealt after 9pm. His client list was a colourful array of professionals from barristers to bankers to MP's. If you lost your job or were falling apart you were off the list. If you were late you were off the list, if you said something Pete didn't like, you were off the list.

His clients bought in advance and in bulk for the weekend, where they would inevitably be hosting an evening. A consignment went something like this:

10 x Eight Ball – Cocaine - £1,200

40 x Large Rock – Crack - £3,200

20 x Large Bag – Heroin - £800

He wasn't your average street dealer and nor were his clients. And business was good, too good to leave alone. You could say he was addicted. Addicted to the money, the criminal aspect, the hero worship he received as his clients fought hard to stay on the list. Deep down somewhere very far away, he knew he couldn't continue, but for now he would push those thoughts away and continue in the name of his children. How honourable!

Pete parked his car a few roads up from where he'd picked it up and went on foot to the first drop. He had six drops to make in three hours and he had set them up to work for both himself and the customer. He'd mostly deal with the errand boys and girls of the bill payers, these would be lovers and hangers on, on the party scene. Desperate young things looking to get high for the cost of being sexually abused. Everyone had their price. He would make the drops and that was it. The payment had already been made using a courier service a few days before. It was by all accounts an extremely successful business. He started to think of Bally and how grateful she would be, when she found out it was him who was helping her. Thoughts of her pushing against his body, happy to be in his arms, his woman. The woman he had rescued, raced across his mind.

A few days earlier off the coast of Essex, Bally's proverbial penny had finally dropped. Blue was not her saviour, in fact what he was, was an abusive motherfucker and she had temporarily lost her mind. Shame washed over her as her memory decided to bring back to life her past ordeal. Her mind who was not her best friend at the moment, was popping up some horribly graphic and horrific images, like flashcards you would use to aid a child's learning. *'Remember this'* her conscience went, *'and this? Hey what about this one?'* There was no escape, in the stone cold light of day, in the harshness of sobriety she was forced to deal with the horror of what had happened to her. Her heart heaved at the memory of numerous vicious rapes,

Nearly Thirteen Months

blurred sexual assaults, drug addiction, her stupidity, her hatred of herself, she hated her mother. The list went on and on, she had started to cry, sometimes in the day as she was just making a tea or sitting reading, or in a session with The Good Doctor as Ann called him.

Big fat wet patches splattered across her cheeks most days and because of this, she decided to drink more water as surely crying this much could leave you seriously dehydrated. Her pitifulness was interspersed with anger, the sort of anger that could fuel a stream train and probably do the same sort of damage, if you were stupid enough to stand in its way. The other residents sensed this and avoided her at all costs. The frail drug dependent weakling and been replaced with a mentally and physically strong nasty bitch. One of the residents had worked in IT and had nicknamed her Snapdragon after the latest super-fast computer processor, the moniker had stuck. Her mind whirred and they joked that you could actually hear it spinning. Ann was the only one who seemed not to mind the acidic remarks.

When she wasn't boohooing she thought about the person who was paying for her to be at Hotel Recovery. Her mind spun because it definitely wasn't that Motherfucker, so if it wasn't him, then who was it? So, one afternoon when The Doc and herself had been having one of their little chats, she plucked up the courage and asked who was footing the bill. Her mouth literally dropped open, upon hearing his answer.

"Pete, Pete my," Her mind tried to connect to some understanding of what the fuck was going on. "My drug dealer, ex drug dealer...you're shitting me! Oh my God, what the fuck! Why?" She was getting screechier and screechier and stopped herself; she didn't want The Doc to see her losing it. In comparison, his melodic low tones, instantly soothed the atmosphere, he was the vocal version of a gentle Vicks chest rubbing.

"You'll have to ask him that yourself. If you want I can let you call him." Until now Bally had had no contact with the outside world, this had suited her. She suddenly wasn't sure if she wanted to contact any one let alone Pete. Errrrr Pete? What the fuck! Why him?

"Not yet, no thank you, I'd like to give it some thought." She'd pulled herself back together scraping composure from places she didn't even know existed. And with her mind in various fragments making a tremendous amount of noise, she gingerly left the room.

She literally didn't know what to think. As she once again found herself leaning up against the oak panelling for support. Images of her flat, the damp patches snaking up the walls, across the yellowy ceiling, sprung to mind as she closed her eyes blocking out ruby red thick brocade curtains, dressing the haughty stained glass window at the end of the corridor. She suddenly felt very sacred, more scared than she had ever been in her entire life. Adrenaline pumped through her, as she stood rooted to the spot. She couldn't move her arms, she was literally scared stiff, gasping for breath. And just then Mrs Potts was by her side, holding one of those small plastic bin bags to her mouth.

"Breath love, just breath. Look at the bag, that's right 1, 2, 3 and in. That's it girl look at the bag and concentrate on me voice. 1, 2, 3 and out 1, 2, 3. That's right love. You're alright darling, you're gonna be alright."

Bally slunk to the floor, with Mrs Potts help and cried like a child, while Mrs Potts held her tight, making sssshing comforting noises.

"Isn't it supposed to be a paper bag?" Bally spluttered a few minutes later.

"Well to be fair, I wan'ed to save me good paper bags for me mushrooms." The uncomfortableness that Bally had felt about being so helpless, needing another human being was instantly brushed over with some good old fashioned English humour and she was grateful for Mrs Potts for taking the bait. Having a last tight hug they scrambled off the floor, with Bally helping the less agile older woman.

"Now if there's nothing else you'll be needin', I'll be off, this place don't run itself." Mrs Potts like all the staff was on strict orders not to interfere with any of the patients care. If there was a problem they were to make sure the patient was Ok and that was it. It was the patient's responsibility to pull themselves together. So she left quickly and didn't look back, even though she was fond of Bally and would have liked to see her to her room and tuck her up by the fire.

Watching Mrs Potts bustle down the corridor and out of view, Bally was once again left with her own thoughts. Ok so now she knew what a panic attack felt like and sent a brief memo to God requesting it never happen again, this is of course the God she didn't believe in.

She took her thoughts back to Pete as she went back to her room. Her body felt heavy, as if the sumptuous carpet was pulling her down, this briefly reminded her of the little girl who went through the tree trunk to sit with the Devil and drink hot chocolate. So it was Pete that was pulling the strings, her strings. What the fuck and why? She needed to talk to him, but was anxious about how he'd perceive her. He must have seen her in that state with Blue, she could hardly bear to think about it. Oh God (him again) how had this all happened to her, why had it all happened? She climbed into bed pulling the enormous duvet over her head and slept. Who knew being clean could be so exhausting?

And it wasn't just physically exhausting, the endless weeks at Hotel Recovery were also taking their toll on Bally's belief system. She spent hours now walking along the beach with Ann discussing their lives. Ann still said she was going to starve herself to death, but when she could safely do it on her own, in her own time. Bally was attempting to break through Ann's bullshit and make her see sense, in this Bally was ruthless. Ann on the other hand was as cool as a cucumber.

"Ann, you fucked up nut job. What the cock are you talking about?" Bally boomed aggressively at her companion. The wind whipping her hair all over the place. She looked wild eyed and mischievous.

"I know you're gonna say, I don't want to do it anymore, but I do." Ann's voice in comparison was warm and compassionate.

"Oh please, please fucking spare me the sob story. If yer were gonna do it, you'd have done it by now? Diiiiiiiscuss?"

"I just want it to be right, timing is everything, when I say goodbye to the physical world."

"Alright Bobby, let's say you do starve yourself to death, what does that exactly mean. I mean what is your fucking protest about?"

'It's about nothing, don't you realise, I just like starving and I'm not dying, more awakening. I'm awakening from this very realistic physical dream. I'm going to enter my consciousness. Diiiiiiscuss that you fucked up junkie cunt!" Ann had learnt a lot from Bally. "Tell me what reality means to you, where is your reality; does such a thing even exist?"

"I can feel it now, I can touch it, when you're dead, your dead. That's it no more feeling. Bye bye world!"

"The world as you know it my friend, the world as you know it! But imagine God, imagine love, that's what God is. When you die you have love. Such love." Ann spoke with such a calm strength, such a knowing, it was as if she knew what she was talking about and this made Bally even more infuriated.

"How the fuck do you know that, How the fuck can you be so sure, what happens if you've got it wrong? Annatha you are proper fuckin deluded!" Bally did not want her newly found friend to die.

"Bally you will never understand without faith and faith is trust in the unknown. And to trust in the unknown, takes immense mental strength. When I'm starving my body I feel closer to God, the real God, the universal God not that Christian numptey. You will always struggle to understand when for the entirety of your life you've been working towards gaining status, having this, grabbing at that. The whole of your adult existence has all been about what you can get and how people perceive you. You're a very shallow human being, who thinks they are deep. I would say it is you who is deluded." Ann breathing steadily starred blissfully at nothing Bally could see. Her face radiated love in the weak September sun, her previous frown and tired skin had been replaced with a slight tinge of pink and her eyes shone the colour of hope. Bally realised Ann had stopped fighting, she was at peace and it crossed her mind she might look exactly this way when laid out in a mortuary slab, which made her shiver.

10 OCTOBER

"The first step towards getting somewhere is to decide you're not going to stay where you are."

John Pierpont 'J.P' Morgan

It was time to go. The Good Doc informed her; she had until the beginning of next month. She was being given a month to reintegrate into society. Four weeks to reach out to the rest of the world. She was to have some visits from those in 'the know' about her stay, a few friends, who knew about the drug bit but nothing else. A few friends? Bally wracked her brain for even one friend that might take an interest in her. The Doc handed her the list, watching her intently.

1) Pete (10am Tuesday)

2) Caroline (10am Wednesday)

3) Api (10am - 1st Nov)

4) Gareth (10am - 2nd Nov)

Bally did one of those quizzical faces which dogs do when they're hoping to get a treat, whilst compiling her own mental list.

1) Pete was coming tomorrow, the Pete who knows all about what happened, who has sorted everything out!

2) Who the fuck was Caroline?

3) Awwwww Api she's such a sweetheart.

4) Sweet Jesus please not Gareth...errrrrr.

"Arghhhhhh Pete, do I have to?"

"Yes Bally you do!" He retorted in a fatherly way. He would miss Bally, in all she'd been one of his more amusing patients. She really was very funny.

"Can't I do the washing up instead?"

"No you can't. Pete is coming and because you're an adult and in control of your own life, you have to be the one to tell him what is on your mind, how you feel, what you want or don't want. By all means when he's here and you don't want to see him, all you have to do is say it to his face." Bally cringed at the thought, crying would be good now, but no tears would come, she must be dehydrated. "And Pete will explain whats been happening to your life on the outside, while you've been in here for three months and the visitors list."

She trudged miserably out of his office, feeling

slightly envious of the posh lot who faced the chopper during the French Revolution, lucky bastards. Ann was waiting for her in the kitchen, they had a 5pm walk scheduled, the day was nearly over and the sky was darkening. Ann patted her mate on the shoulder as she held the door open, oh dear someone has bad news. Taking the lead, Bally breathed in the damp chilly air, it hurt in that nice way, made her feel alive. They walked in silence, Ann waiting until Bally spoke, she knew she would just needed a little time, that's what was good about being at Hotel Recovery you had a lot of time.

"I'm being turned out." Ann noted her friend's use of vocabulary. "I'm being let go, P45 time, no longer wanted, surplus to requirements, I'm like a 1980's coal miner."

Ann could barely suppress her laughter. "Feeling a little rejected are we?"

"Yes, but I'm not quite sure what from. I know that doesn't make sense. I know I've got to face the world at some point I just don't want to do it ….arghhhh and Pete's coming tomorrow."

"Pete your ex-dealer, the one who's footing the bill?"

"Yes Peter my supposed hero, my rock. I should be grateful, but I can't feel gratitude for something that's so fucked up. I know he knows what happened to me. It's the knowing that's killing me. All that information in the public domain…arghhhhhhh! Bally had started waving her arms about and Ann pulled back a little to avoid being whacked in the face as they headed for the shore. The sun had gone, but there was still a glow to the west, the sky was beautiful, a bright blue waiting to get darker. Stopping so their boots were just inches from the lapping water they stood in silence until Ann spoke. "Take it one day at a time, speak to Pete, nothing bad can happen, yes you have your shame, but shame doesn't like being out in the open. Once you've spoken to Pete you'll feel better."

"Arghhhhh…I hate facing things, I won't even know what to say. I mean, you'd understand if you'd seen how I acted around him, just desperate to get him to like me, so needy, so pathetic. Arghhhh I just hate myself for it, it's so embarrassing."

"Well I didn't say it would be easy."

"No you spouted some 'one day at a time' bullshit. No one in crisis wants to hear that shite. No one! And I am in crisis. My names Bally and I'm in cunting crisis. There must me a helpline somewhere. Crisis Cunting Anonymous CCA? Have you got the number, you look like the type of fuckin delinquent that would be calling."

"Miiiiiaoooow… pussy cat!" Anns response was

light hearted but firm. "Put those horrid little talons of yours away, there's no point in getting bitchy with me. I didn't make this happen, you did and the sooner you accept that and drop the poor me routine the better for all of us."

Bally looked glum, she hated being told off, it reminded her of her relationship with her mother. She knew she should apologise, but her ego wanted to continue. She had no idea why she was behaving like such a bitch and then she said it.

"Fuck off and die Ann." The silence that ensued was so heavy it could have sunk one of the freight ships that they were so fond of watching. Bally immediately regretted opening her mouth, but it was too late the words were out. Ann had turned and was walking back alone and Ballys pride wouldn't let her chase after her and beg for forgiveness. She stood there impotent, what had she just done? She hardly recognised herself. Why was she being so mean, especially to Ann the only person she had ever been really close to. The only person who had ever seen her wobble, seen her vulnerable.

It was pitch black outside when Bally crept up the dimly lit staircase cold and miserable. She had missed dinner with the others and knew there would be a cold plate of meat and cheese in her room. She didn't care, she wasn't hungry anyway, she felt sick, worn out, confused. She had had

Nearly Thirteen Months

no peace as she'd crisscrossed across the island marching to the most horrific thoughts, where her Mother kept begging her to come home, back to her little girl room, that had not changed since she was ten. Her room all pink with overstuffed animals and posters of horses. What the fuck was that all about? Desperate to find peace she battled her way through the sand dunes and drifts, just keep going her mind told her, run and it will soon go away. But it hadn't, her mother's face leapt out at her from the reflection in her bedroom window. Fuck she was properly losing her mind. Her mother's taunting words echoed in her head... *'No one wants you, not even nice Ann. Did you think she liked you? Oh poor silly child, no one likes you because you're difficult, you were always difficult, difficult and selfish.'* The words kept coming and she was desperate for some emotional pain relief. Lying on the bed she curled up into a ball, she knew no little helpers were on their way, there was nothing else for her to do.

All the while the Doc was sitting at his desk thinking. Ann had come hours earlier to tell him about Bally being on the brink and that she was scared she was gonna do something stupid. Ironic coming from Ann he thought. He knew both women were healing and they had to go through the darkness on their own. It was a brutal harsh reality, but one they both had to face. He knew Bally wouldn't kill herself. Bally had unfinished business, she was far too angry to top herself. There was something wrong though. She was angry, that was a good sign. Angry meant she was acknowledging what had happened to her but she was so locked in emotionally, that he wondered if she'd survive on the outside after one bout of rehab. He doubted it very much. Most of his patients had been in numerous facilities before they landed on his couch, it was the last stop for many, they knew it and so did he.

Bally had never confronted any of her emotions and had spent a life time hiding from them since she was a young child. She literally didn't know how to feel, to feel sad when something was wrong, happy when she did well. Mrs Potts had come to report that Bally's dinner was untouched and she was lying in the foetal position looking like a baby who was worn out from being over stimulated. Mrs Potts did have a way with words he mused and in her defense very rarely got it wrong about the patient's mental states, the woman really was worth her weight in gold. So here was this young woman in her early 30's unable to apologise to a friend and simply say sorry for saying something she didn't mean. All this drama for that, no wonder the girl was exhausted.

The Doc went to bed that night with his thoughts elsewhere. The woman Caroline who had called to set up a meeting with Bally had definitely been the one who had dropped her off all battered and bruised just a few months ago; he'd recognise her voice anywhere. He had sort of let her pass through his mind knowing that nothing would ever come of his feelings towards this unusual female, who had so piqued his masculine spirit. She had been breathy on the call and he'd sensed the intimacy between them and not wanted her to end their conversation. And now she would be back, coming back and he would not let her go this time. The night passed slowly, full of dreams of passion and friendship. When the morning came he did not want to wake.

Earlier on that same night Bally lay hiding under the covers, it could be worse she thought, oh fuck cunting shite it was. Pete was coming tomorrow and not just tomorrow anytime he was gonna be in front of her in the morning. Mr fastidious time keeper, arghhhhh she wouldn't even have the pleasure of a tardy turn up. Fuck, fuck, fuck, please God let me not wake up! Let me die in a freak heart attack, not wake up stroke thingy! Please God hear my prayers, she chanted until falling fast asleep, totally exhausted.

He obviously hadn't been listening as the dawn dawned and the birds chorused and the weak sun was getting out of bed the same time Bally's eyes flittered open. Oh fuck christ, literally fuck you God you cunt. I'm still alive, thanks for that one mate. No wonder no one believes any more with that sort of response rate. You're a right proper cunt!

Blaspheming always put Bally in a good mood and she continued shouting 'God you're a cunt' as she showered and ran down for brekkie in the big kitchen to face the others who by this time would all know Pete was coming. But unbeknown to her God had been listening and had decided to gift her with a full eight hours sleep which had done her the world of good. It had given her an energy and a vibrancy about her that you could say made her shine. With freshly washed hair framing her little face, tight faded blue jeans and soft cream wool jumper she looked very beautiful. Her blues eyes sparkled with mischief as she clocked Ann. The other residents looked on apprehensively; a visit was a big thing at Hotel Recovery.

"Good morning comrades!" Bally stood in front of her slightly fearful audience. "I would like to take this opportunity to apologise for my cunty behaviour over the last few months. I am truly sorry and Ann I am especially sorry for the way I spoke to you yesterday, there is no excuse and it won't happen again." Bally held her head high, her voice was strong and purposeful, she was enjoying herself. "As you all know, as you're all a pile of gossiping shysters, I have a visit this morn. My visitor is due in 51 minutes. I am slightly nervous, but would like to share the following: Pete was my drug dealer and I behaved in a sexually depraved desperate way every time I saw him, which unfortunately, was quite often. I am deeply ashamed by my behaviour and now have to face him. I feel sick, but I'm going to do it. Thank you for listening." And with that she slumped into the nearest chair as the room exploded into thunderous applause and whooping!

Ann came to sit next to her pushing a bacon sandwich and cup of tea her way.

"Well that was errrrr revealing." Her impression of her friend was quite good. Bally leant over and hugged her. Hugged her tight and whispered in her hair.

"50 minutes to go."

"Actually, it's 49."

"Arghhhhh, and the mother fucker is always on time."

"What?" Ann looked her in disbelief. "On time? I thought he was a drug dealer? On time? I've never heard anything so preposterous in all my born days. Utterly ridiculous." And she kept up the banter and they chatted anxiously for that's what was needed at this time, until they heard a car pull up and Bally looked like she was going to puke.

"OK Bally Dancer this is it. It's your big day, you get to walk out on your own and show the world and yourself how strong your spine is, so pecker up girl and do what you've got to do." And with that she literally dragged the wobbling Bally to her feet and pushed her in the direction of the great hall, also known as the front door. The grandfather clock chimed telling anyone who cared, it was ten o'clock as the doorbell rang through the house into the kitchen on its old fashioned wire. Ding dong, brriing brriing, ding dong the bells rang simultaneously as Bally opened the door.

As the huge door swung open Pete couldn't believe his eyes, her hair was short, it made her look like a naughty little pixie, a very beautiful naughty pixie. He took her all in, the beautiful shiny hair, sparkling blue eyes that looked straight into his, small breasts hidden in a soft jumper, slim lean strong legs in tight faded flared blue jeans and were those moccasins? Blimey she looked like someone from a 1970's Country Magazine. He spoke first.

"'ello girl, and how's my Bally Dancer?" His voice was so London, it startled her, he didn't belong here. She did, he didn't.

"Errrrrrr," Oh for fuck's sake not that again. She cleared her throat and tried again. "I'm well Pete, thank you for asking. Please come in." She was in control and she lead him through to the drawing room (the place where you sat with visitors). The fire had been lit recently, the logs were fresh, it looked staged, sort of not real. The whole room was too tidy, Bally thought as she went to sit

Nearly Thirteen Months

down on the sofa and beckoned for Pete to sit opposite her on the armchair. There was a smallish round table between them, carved wood with a beautiful mosaic tiled surface in red and yellow. Pete noticed her looking at it as she traced her finger over the bumps.

"Bally I've come to make you an offer and I'd like you to think about it for a bit before you give me an answer...I'm also gonna tell you a bit about 'ow you got 'ere." She nodded in agreement and as he spoke her mind whirred, she couldn't believe what she was hearing, she looked away as her mind raced on. And to top it all off, he was so good looking it made her fanny ache. She couldn't believe she fancied him so much. He looked calm and purposeful, masculine and sexy. They we're briefly interrupted some ten minutes later as Mrs Potts brought tea in and quietly left them to it.

"Shall I be Mum then?" And as she went to pour tea they both knew at that point the deal was done. Pete had said his bit and she had listened.

"No ta, I've gotta shoot." He came over to her and cupped one hand around her face lifting her chin to kiss her gently on the side of her mouth. It was all so slow and deliberate; Bally touched his hand as they looked into each other's eyes. And then that was it and she watched him walking off and not looking back as he closed the door, which made a loud clunk. It reminded her of a jail door being bolted shut in an old Alcatraz movie she'd watched years ago.

Pete pulled up in front of the causeway and took a piss onto the pebbles beneath him. He felt good, pissing outside in the fresh air always felt good. Bally had felt good, she had not disappointed, his thoughts went to the softness of her face, her lips. Demure and beautiful, was what she was and he had saved her. He felt his whole body tingle as good old testosterone pumped alongside adrenaline, fueling his ego, his masculinity. Her strength of mind and poise had pleased him, she had not begged for more clarification and had listened intently. She was not some hysterical whining woman, she was in control and he liked that about her. He liked himself even more for picking a winner like her. He happily congratulated himself on the choice he had made. Back in the car his mind went in the direction of the house they would live in together, with her waiting for him when he came home. The vintage photo filter he was processing all thoughts of Bally through, was working overtime. Click, click it went, on a continuous reel.

Bally sat for some time where Pete had left her, trying to get a handle on what he had said. She was literally blown away. Wow what an offer, don't fuckin' worry about anything, I'll sort it all out for you. Who the fuck was he? She had literally been too shocked to speak. He talked about her old flat and that Blue had done a runner. He said he'd had Crystal sort through all her stuff and move it in to storage and that he had sublet the flat to a weird Bulgarian couple, so the rent was all paid if she ever wanted to go back.

Crystal had talked to her mum and everyone and said that she was in rehab and that she'd come tomorrow and explain further. *Ahhhh Caroline, that Crystal, she'd ask her in person about the name change.* He said she needed looking after and that he had daughters that were looking forward to seeing her and that she could convalesce in a beautiful county home, his home. She'd be looked after. She'd be part of a family who cared for her. That he had always cared for her. Her desperate need for someone to love her, her desire to be taken care of and cherished caused an actual physical pain in her chest.

She suddenly felt very much in need. Feeling small and frightened, thinking she was unable to care for herself, she knew she would agree. She just didn't have the strength to stand on her own, he would look after her, he had said so. She was going to be cared for and with those thoughts rushing around her head she bolted out the door to find Ann who happened to be sitting on the staircase waiting for her.

"And?" Ann's face was alight with excitement; she already had her coat and boots on and was hurrying Bally to do the same. Walking briskly down to the beach Bally retold the account of Pete's visit. It took about half a second for Ann's face to go from emoji smiley to emoji angry. She breathed deeply trying not to get defensive and shouty. What the fuck was this guy trying on? Bally was just about to walk herself into a whole pile of shit. But instead she said. "Oh wow it's a lot to take in, it's good he gave you a bit of time to think about it, when you gonna give him your answer?"

"I already have."

"It's quite a big decision, maybe have a sleep on it."

"Why, what for? He's really helped me out. I mean, without him I would have been dead."

"You don't know that for starters and for seconders you don't owe him anything." Ann turned to her friend, mentally willing her to wake the fuck up. Bally looked across at the worried face and found herself getting slightly irritated about Ann's moral high-ground.

"I'm on my fuckin' own, I've got nowhere to go. I'm not gonna marry the bloke, just sit tight for a bit and get better…isn't that what everyone wants me to do?" Bally had a defense that was impossible to break and they both knew it.

"Yes love, 'cause it is, you know what you're doing. Good luck I'm sure everything will be fine, more than fine." And with that they linked arms and wandered off down the beach bumping into each other on purpose and smirking.

It was already time for Bally's next visit and this time she sat on the old cast iron bench by the front door waiting for Crystal. The weak autumn sun shone down on her upturned face, as her mind went over the times they'd spent together. She'd only ever seen Crystal when they were doing drugs together, and suddenly the fear gripped her, maybe Crystal wouldn't like the new boring Bally, the insecure, needy, can't stand on her own two feet, drip. As she was mentally slapping herself down Crystal drove up the long curved drive and clocked her old mucker. Getting out of the car she was immediately taken back at the transformation of the woman that stood in front of her. They hugged awkwardly pulled away then tried again and this time it worked and they held on patting each other on the back.

"Oh dearie me, what have you got on your feet?" Crystal questioned as she looked from her own well shod leather ankle boots to Bally's.

"They're Moccasins. Historically, the footwear of the indigenous people of North America."

"Hmmmmm, its nah wonder them cowboys wan'ed ter shot 'em."

"Because they had the wrong footwear?"

"Well *wrong* is bein' nice, to be fair." Crystal looked into Ballys eyes. "You look good hun, you look well. You should be proud of yerself." Bally struggling under the intensity of Crystals glare shifted from Moccasin to Moccasin. Unable to look up she found herself stifling back the sobs. "Oh just fuckin' cry will yer, I mean if yer gonna do it, do it inside, I need a pee." Crystal had started to jiggle.

"I've been wondering about the effects of extensive sobbing on the body's homeostasis."

"Frickin' rivetin', in the meantime please don't explain what homeo whatever is and take me to the fuckin' toilet. Focus gurl, keep walkin', that's right."

Bally watched her tall and slender friend stalk off in the direction of the little ladies room and mused over her feline like sway, her body literally purred along, like some beautifully maintained classic automobile. Crystal looked so sassy, so in control and she wondered what was really going on in her head for her to be trying so hard to look so well balanced. Fake it to make it eh! Bally was all eyes and ears as she waited patiently.

They decided to make tea and Bally led the way to the upstairs snug which faced East. The sun just about made it through the pained glass floor to ceiling windows, as they sat on two gorgeously comfy armchairs facing out across the dunes. It was a beautiful, cosy room, with loads of magazines and blankets slung everywhere. A calm and peaceful place, Crystal thought as she took in her surroundings.

"What's with the Caroline bit then?"

"Ahhh I 'ad a sort of midlife crisis when I made the call to the big boss 'ere."

"I'm all ears."

"I dunno, it just came out."

"A Freudian slip?"

"Sumfink like that." Bally watched her friend look out across the dunes wistfully, everything about her was immaculate, poised, regulated.

"What are you thinking about now?" She asked gently.

"Why I'd want the big boss 'ere to know my real name? I never use it, no one does. It don't make sense. Not much does any more."

"I'm with you on that one Caroline, reality is a real head fuck."

"I like you saying Caroline."

"Then I shall say it more often, just to please you." As she spoke she laid her hand over her friends arm and gave it a little squeeze, taking note of Crystal's aka Caroline's rapid change of subject.

"Thanks hun." She smiled and began." I need to tell you what's been goin' on regarding your family, friends and flat and all that jazz. I 'ad your phone and got all your numbers and told everyone who needed to know that you were gonna be out of commission for six months. I told 'em all that it was a well posh place and work was paying for it and that you couldn't talk to anyone. Your mum went into one, somefink 'bout your dad's blood pressure and shame, bless her."

"That was too be expected, she's quite selfless, in fact even Mother Theresa used to go to her for advice."

"Yeah, I remember you saying that before." As soon as she spoke she locked eyes with Bally and smiled conspiratorially with her. They had had some good times. Some very good times. "So everyone got a kind of different story to who was coughing up the dollar, but basically everyone thinks you've had a difficult time coping with drug addiction, pressures of work, family, morons etc. and that you went away to recover and now you're makin' a 'Kylie come back', all clean and fuckin' serene. Oh yeah and I dumped Mr Wrong for ya, you can thank me later for that one."

"That was very kind of you, really just too kind." As they discussed Bally's life like she was a per-

Nearly Thirteen Months

son on the witness protection scheme, Caroline thought of Pete and how this was all a bit weird.

"Bally hun let me talk to you about Pete. Woz goin on there mate?"

"What Mr I wanna save Princess Bally from herself?"

"Yeah, well that's a good start. Dya not think it's slightly frickin' weird? A little bit controlling on a fuckin' enormous scale? I mean he wants you to go shack up with him and his kids in some fuck off country pad."

"Yes I do think its slightly unusual."

"Slightly unusual? Bally he's not some ole Aunt, he woz our fuckin' dealer. He's the man that has sorted all this out." Pointing wildly at the ceiling, floor, walls. "Dya not fink he's gonna want somfink back?"

"Calm down Cryst..errrr Caroline, you're right, of course you're right, I'm not fuckin' stupid. I know what he wants and he can have it. Don't you get it I need somewhere to go. I can't be back in London on my own. I need him, I need his help."

"Alwight gurl, easy, I'm sorry." And at that point she truly was. Sorry for the whole fuck up which was all of their lives. She knew Bally was going with Pete and she was gonna have a fuck load of trouble.

"Caro can I ask you something?" Bally was already struggling with the syllable count in Caroline.

"Ahhemmm knock yourself out." She said clearing her throat and sitting back in the armchair.

"What happened to the boy?" Bally watched her intently and saw the tiny flinch at the corner of her eye when it happened, just in the crease, hardly noticeable. She'd been watching for a sign and there it was.

"Pete told me he roughed him up a bit, well quite badly actually. He sort of gave him a good kicking and that was that, never seen again. He's had your flat done up and is keeping up with the rent." There she went again with the change of subject. Bally was noting everything, something wasn't right, but she wasn't gonna get it out of Crystal or whatever her fuckin' name was, well not now, not today."

They chatted and went down for lunch and Bally kept hold of her suspicions and Caroline kept her thoughts about Pete to herself. And then The Doctor walked in. "Good afternoon ladies?" It was a question and Caroline answered.

"Yes it is, well all thirty minutes of it." She said glancing up at the clock. What the fuck thought Bally as she eyed up her mate, oh my god Cryst/Caro was flirting with the Doc. Oh my god and he was flirting back. Shit when did this happen, what the fuck, this was too good!

"Errrrrr Caroline let me just get my boots and we can go for a walk, give me a minute I'll just run upstairs."

"I thought we were having something to eat I'm starving?"

"Bally aren't those your boots by the door?" The Doctor butted in.

"No, yes… I want the other ones." She yelped as she ran off in the direction of her room stomping as loudly as possible.

On their own in the kitchen, the atmosphere changed in a heart beat. The air between them crackled with the electrical current of a storm on biblical proportions. Neither spoke, their eyes locked, reading each others minds. Neither can remember how it happened as they found themselves a breath away from each other's lips. And then he kissed her. And she kissed him back as Bally who'd done a 180 on the landing and tiptoed her way back, watched on from the doorway.

Bally could not tear herself away. She'd just been about to walk in when she saw the Doc stride the few feet between them and hold on the Caroline's waist with both hands and push his face down on to hers. With her back arched, she responded with a passion and gentleness that made Bally envious.

They looked beautiful and yes she was jealous. She backed out from the doorway and shouted from the corridor. "I've got my boots, Caro you ready?" counting to three before she entered the room, as a rather flustered Doctor hurried out the door past her.

Caro stood open mouthed where he had left her. "Oh my frickin' Jesus Christs all rolled into one, you and the Good Doctor were just tonguing each other, swapping saliva stories, investigating each other's oral plaque." And with that they both burst out laughing.

"An' I'd like to report his oral plaque is quite something." Caroline fired back.

"Oh my giddy ya! You just snogged the frickin Doctor."

"Yeah and I liked it," she sang mimicking that Katy Perry song with a massive smile on her face.

"We must celebrate with some leftover chicken pie and a herbal tea. We must mark the occasion." Bally's tone was drafted from a BBC news reader.

"Fuck that's too much…no I couldn't possibly…ok let's do it, let's cut open a frickin' chickin pie..woo hoo!"

And they hugged each other tight and held on for dear life, each frightened to let go first and both for very different reasons.

11 NOVEMBER

"It's exhausting being me, as everytime I wake I know I will have to spend the whole day with myself."

Jane De Croos, Author

The countdown to her own deportation had been filled with a horrid gnawing feeling that she was making a big mistake. Unfortunately, she had neither courage nor humility to admit to herself that being carried away by Pete on his trusty delusion was of any benefit to either party involved. She heaved a heavy sigh and waited for Api to pitch, she'd been waiting half an hour already.

The hallway was dark and unlit which mirrored her sombre mood. She'd been seeing the Doc three times a week in the last month and knew that he thought she was making a big mistake as well, even though he would never say it to her face, she just couldn't pull out now. He'd advised his client that Bally was not ready but Pete was confident that if things didn't work out she could come back. And the customer is always right.

Why couldn't she just put a stop to it all she didn't know? She was totally drained by the fear of leaving Hotel Recovery, being out there in the big wide world without any support, drained and tired from just being alive.

The front door bell jangled aggressively causing her to jump out of her skin, she must have dozed off. For a moment she didn't know why she was sitting on the stairs in the hallway, like that green frog from 'whats that program called?' She couldn't remember, she'd started recently to forget all sorts of things like names of places and people. Luckily, she remembered her next visitor's moniker and as the bell rang again, she called out, "Hi Happy." Forcing out a bit of bravado!

"Oh my god, it's really you!" Api stood in the doorway taking in the picture of health that stood in front of her. "You look just beautiful, really well, really, really well."

Bally bowed her head full of a shame that just wouldn't go away.

"Awww you were always so kind to me, thank you." And she meant it. The women took each other in as they headed arm in arm for the kitchen. "Did you get here alright on the train? The Doc said they would send a bloke for you at the station."

"Yes, he was very lovely and had a sign just in case I forgot my own name!" Api laughed out loud, a deep, harmonic boom blowing the dust off the old tapestries in the gloomy corridor.

They were soon eating buttery crumpets chitty chatting about everything, Api looked both sad and concerned whilst, Bally did her best to brush off Api's constant questioning regarding Pete. Unlike The Good Doc, she felt no need to keep her own council. "So you, Bally who needs to be very careful and take very good care of herself is just gonna go shack up with a guy who seems to be quite a bit controlling to me. I mean...can you not hear the alarm bells going madam...eh misses? There's no such thing as favours like this, from men like him. He'll have you paying sooner or later! Come on girlie, wakey wakey. Why don't you come stay with me until you're back on your little Bally feet?" Api had laid her hands on Bally's forearms and at one point during the lecture she thought Api was actually going to forcibly shake her. Api on the other hand, was doing her best not to slap her incredibly hard into the next week.

After about two long and arduous hours, Api gave up her London Inquisition, heaved a great sigh and slumped back in an other overstuffed armchair, the house was full of them, Bally mused, looking on, somewhat concerned by the woman in front of her. Only someone who was struggling in their own personal life would worry or feel the need to judge another so vehemently as Api had just done. She watched Api's eyes dart to the floor bringing sadness to the room.

"Api, why don't you tell me what's up?" Bally's voice was full of warmth and love. The gentleness of Bally's voice took Api totally off guard instantly, and her eyes suddenly filled with tears that rolled down smooth cheeks, leaving a silvery trail. Sniffing hard, dabbing her cheeks with a rather manky tissue, Api attempted to speak, but no words came. Her body heaved as she desperately tried to choke back the flood gates that Bally had nudged open with her kind words.

Going over to her and perching on the chair's arm she buried Api's head into her oversized knit jumper whilst stroking her hair and making soothing shushy noises. It was quite a while before Api managed to get herself under control, but she did and Bally, so as not to embarrass her, got up to put the kettle on. As she was clanking around the Aga, Api spoke, her voice cold and bitter, horribly out of place in the cosy kitchen.

"I can't conceive. We've been trying for three years now. I can't have children. I get my period every month. Tom doesn't want to do IVF, he says he's not bothered. I've never spoken to anyone about this." It was out, she'd done it. Now the cold harsh facts of her barren womb were in the public domain, she would be pitied by her family, friends and associates alike. They would all find out, feel sorry for her and her pathetic attempts to get pregnant. Advice would come tumbling in from do-gooders. Leave Tom! Find a man that wants what you want! Not everyone is blessed with offspring! Tom's a good man isn't that enough? He loves you! You love him don't you? She could hear their overbearing voices full of judgement as her mental list went on.

Bally handed Api a cup of tea and sat down to watch the woman in front of her trying to make sense of the unfair world she'd been placed in. With hands clenched tightly around her miserable, sodden tissue, Api trembled slightly, her downcast eyes swollen and puffy. She didn't look up as Bally spoke.

"I'm so sorry Aps what a horrible place for you to be in and with no one to talk to, I'm sorry I was never there for you, I truly am. But I'm here now and I'm glad you could feel you could tell me." Api sniffed loudly in response keeping her eyes glued to the tiled floor. "Now it's out, why don't you tell me more about how you feel. Like how long have you wanted to be pregnant and have you had any tests done?"

Api finally looked up and sighed, it was as if all the tension had been squeezed out of her. "I'm so sorry Bally I'm supposed to be here for you, helping you. It's just been so stressful; I've not been able to think of anything else now for three years. I thought it would be so easy, I'd come off the pill and whoop whoop I'd be a bun in the oven carrier, easy as lemon meringue pie!

And then the months rolled on and every time I get my period, it's like mamma nature saying look at you, you nothing but a failure, you're no woman, you'll never be a mamma. I just can't cope any more. I just can't see my period every month, I want a baby so much now Bally it hurts me physically, I have pain in my chest, it hurts so much. Why can't I have a baby growing inside of me, like all those other mamma's around? All I see now is pregnant women and I hate them, I just hate them!" Api's voice was so full of grief that it took Bally all of her strength not to cry along with her.

As Api poured her heart out, Bally pondered how very wrong she had got the 'happy Api'. If only she'd taken a moment to ask the woman in front of her who had always been so kind to her, how she really was, but she hadn't. She had been a really shitty friend and wondered why people were bothering to be with her now. Here they were now though and this was her opportunity to right the wrongs that she had executed in the past. She spoke to Api without emotion. "Sweetheart, listen to me for just one minute, I've got a solution for you, well in fact several." Api looked up at

Bally's smirking face, what was it about Miss Cassey that always intrigued her?

"I'm all ears girl!" Loud sniff!

"First, I need a bit more info, you cool with me asking some questions?" Api nodded her consent. "Do you want to be pregnant or do you want a baby? Think a few years down the line, what's more important to you in let's say three years' time?"

"I want a baby." Api was threatening to blub again, Bally would have to be quick.

"Api this is no time to be crying, you've done enough of it, now it's time to take action, do you agree?"

A slightly shocked Api agreed as Bally continued. "Many women and men suffer with fertility issues and you don't necessarily have to have IVF, but you do need to see a doctor, both of you do and check out what's wrong, if anything. That's the solution."

"Thats it!" Api looked a bit disappointed.

"Yes that's it and when you both get the results back, we'll find solution number two. Api have faith my dear friend, have faith. I know Tom will do as you ask, go privately it will be quicker."

"Ok I'm going to do that and Tom will do it."

"Just tell him that you want him, and you want a baby with him, and then leave it at that."

"Ok, I won't moan on at him.'

"No don't moan, he's probably just as anxious as you are. Get the results and then you can talk." Bally felt a cosmic shift in Api's mood. She pulled her on to her feet and hugged her. "Oh Happy yer big banana, what have you been doing!" Api was beginning to understand how silly she had been, burying her head in the sand. She'd been so frightened, so frightened of it not happening, what other people would think of her.

"Bally, Bally, thank you so much, I needed to hear that, I don't know what I've been doing. I've been a real twit. Your right girl, I gotta take control. Can't wait to tell Tom, I know we can make something happen. I just know it!"

"Blimey, you've changed yer tune…hahha! Good on yer girl!"

The girls chatted about babies and Api only mentioned the Pete thing once again. She wasn't happy about Ballys choice in fact, she thought she was mad, but she also knew she would have to tread her own path. She had said what was needed to be said. As they parted she held her hands. "Bally you know I'll always have your back. Can I come visit you in the Manor House? You leave here next week don't you?"

"Thanks Aps I know you do, you've been a good friend to me, a really good friend. And thanks for coming here today and of course I'd love to see you, when I'm Lady of the house and entertaining guests." The light hearted content, didn't shrug of the ill ease they both felt of Bally living with Pete.

"And you have been a good friend to me my dear, thank you for today." As Api left she begun to understand her shame of not conceiving, that was all it was. God she'd been a real idiot, she could kick herself but smiled instead as she got her lift to the train station. She'd make this work, she was braver now. And look at Bally doing so well, she was so pleased for her and couldn't wait to see her again. Bally was one of those special people and counted her blessings for ever getting to meet her. Life was gonna get loads better for them both, she was sure of that.

When they parted company and Bally had never felt the need to get off her tits, as much as she did right at that moment. She'd had some bad times since she'd come to Hotel Recovery, but this was different. All of a sudden her resolve left her, literally fucked off leaving her with herself and the stark basic facts that she couldn't cope. It rose in her like the rage of a madman, uncontrolled and fierce. Gnawing at her gut and throat, she could taste the vodka, the burn, she could smell the crack, the plastic, the hit was incredible, her desire almost a primal scream.

Clutching her stomach she bolted to the toilet and threw up all over the seat and floor. Leaning against the wall, panting heavily she knew she was gonna have to be very careful, to not fall foul to the dreaded relapse. That night the full moon shone brightly in the cloudless sky, as Bally tossed in her bed, wrapping up her secret in the numerous bed sheets.

The morning crawled in with Bally under the covers. Ann had joined her and was sitting in the armchair pretending to read whilst throwing biscuits into the fire and watching them sizzle. Bally was set to leave tomorrow and her mood was sombre. Caroline would collect her in the morning and take her to Pete's new house, the one he shared with his daughters. Mrs Potts had donated a little old brown leather suitcase to put the few possessions she had in. It reminded Ann of the railway children being evacuated from London during the war. The mood stayed dark, Ann knew Bally wouldn't change her mind, so she talked of the time when they first met and what she thought of her.

"You were sooo stuck up, Miss I'm so much better than the rest of you." Her tone was an attempt at being lighthearted. Bally smiled glad of the break from her incessant thoughts, her mind was not her friend at the moment.

"It wasn't difficult to place myself above such

freaks, present company included of course!"

"And how would you place yourself now, Miss Perfect?"

"Surrounded by my closest friends, somewhere very near the bottom! I aspire to the dregs of society! I can now safely say the only way is up! Underclass here I come! And I know Ann you're right there beside me and I thank you for that..." her voice trailed off and the sadness that had never left the room, only slunk into a corner, rose again now with even more vigour. Fixing her gaze on the burning logs Ann spoke into the fire.

"I don't know what I'm going to do without you."

"You're going to do all the things you usually do."

"Yes that's right, of course I am and you don't need to hear my shit now."

"Well I don't mind to be fair, as it's a break from hearing my own, so go ahead knock yourself out."

"No Bally I won't, I've learnt a lot from you and one of the things I most like about you is your ability to keep your mouth shut."

"I too treasure that quality in myself, and what I like about you is that you're so very kind."

"Kind? Can't I be something more exciting?"

"No you fuckin' can't." She yelled laughing and

with that flung the covers off. "I've got my last visitor, I've got Gareth my boss on his way. I need to mentally and physically prepare, the last time I saw him I had a speech impediment, I need to get my vocal cords in order.

Then my last sess with Doctor Schaffhausen (said in a german accent, they'd been watching old DVD's and Dirty Rotten Scoundrel's was a house favourite) Will you stay with me here whilst I get ready and maybe we can go for a walk together our last one after lunch?" Ann nodded they both knew she would.

Gareth had managed to tread in cat or fox shit on his way up to the big house and was cursing under his breath, he was also late and hated the countryside. The fiercely cold wind whipped against his London clobber, threatening to tear it to shreds if he hung around. Don't worry he thought as soon as he'd seen 'employee of the month' he'd be back to the comforts of the modern world.

Gareth had been thinking a lot about Bally, he was as loyal as they came, true East End boy. He'd heard from her friend Caroline that she was on the mend and would need her job back very soon. He'd heard from Api about Ballys plan to move in with some psycho controlling nut job, one thing he knew was that she needed to be back at work where he could keep an eye on her. Their meet went well, she looked sensational, too well he mused as he was back in the car. Everything was just that little bit too ok. He'd known quite a few close friends do a stint in rehab, none of them were ok after a few months. Bally was faking recovery big time.

Bally eyed Gareth knowing he thought she was a mad and desperate going off to shack up with Pete but he held his tongue as he discussed her route back to gainful employment. Making all the right sounds and gestures she knew then that she'd never go back, waving goodbye to Gareth glad she'd never have to see him again. God why was she being such a bitch? Who fuckin knew? All she knew was she was leaving.

The Good Doctor was in his usual position, at his desk staring out to sea when Bally knocked.

"Come in Bally."

"How do you know it's me?"

"Because you have never been late not once in all the months you've been here. Not by one minute. Or a minute early. Why is that?"

"Are you asking me why I'm punctual?

"I wouldn't call being Greenwich Mean Time on all occasions just 'punctual.'

"Well what would you call it." Bally had a way with words that always left him doing the talking, she really was a skilled linguist he thought, giving himself a moment to answer her. He'd learnt over the years he'd spent with all sorts of patients that the best policy was honesty.

"I'd call it being a perfectionist and never wanting to displease me in any way. You want to show me you're in control and that you are coping and that all is well. Putting that much effort into just being on time and it must take considerable effort to always be bang on the minute shows me that something is wrong. I hear alarm bells tolling from the rafters, ding, dong, ding, dong, they clang. And now you tell me...what's your intuition saying?"

"I don't know what it's saying, I can't hear it with all that clanging going on, but I can hear my mind telling me to be strong and brave."

"I feel your mind might not be being doing the best by you right now. I mean, would you tell anyone in your position to be strong and brave?"

"And what is my position Doc?" There she went again with the red herring, he would not fight her.

"It is whatever you choose it to be, whatever you choose it to be when you are ready to make a choice."

She kept her cool and changed the subject. She'd learnt over their time together that she would not rattle him and she wondered why she always wanted to get one over on him anyway. It all seemed sort of childish now. Her whole existence seemed so very childish now. They talked about her leaving and as they parted after a heart felt hug, the Doc went to stand behind his desk and glancing up to look at Bally who already had her hand on the door knob said. "Come back if you need to, you can always come back, there will be no cost." There was the briefest of silences as if Bally was digesting his words before she replied.

"I won't be coming back." She closed the door gently behind her and she was gone and he knew she meant it.

Ann was waiting in the kitchen to embark on their last walk together, it was cold and miserable and so were they. Neither women bothered to speak, there was nothing to say. They walked as usual down to the beach to stand in front of the dark water. In the distance a large vessel could be seen making its way out to the open sea. Bally focused upon it and relief flooded over her.

She would be free from all this shit she had endured here. She could and would very shortly, do as she pleased. Gareth was keen to have her back at work and maybe she would swallow the shame, knuckle down and do the job she was supposed to. Pete's would just be a bridging pad until she was on her feet. It would be fine, she just had to get on with it all.

Noticing a hardening in Bally's stature Ann placed a hand on her shoulder, more for her own comfort then Bally's. What was any of them doing anyway, she was in no position to judge anyone. They slowly, snaked their way across the island numerous times stopping at all their favourite places, until it got too cold and Bally suggested a hot chocolate that she would make for herself whilst her comrade would have a no calorie herbal tea.

Her last supper was uneventful, she could imagine what it was like for death row inmates as the clock ticked on. There was nothing to do now but wait. Her fate had been sealed she would be leaving tomorrow. Leaving the safety of Hotel Recovery, The Good Doctor, Mrs Potts, Ann and the rest of the inmates. She didn't want to go, she also didn't want to stay. Her mind was doing that thing when it just went off on a tangent on its own.

The young boy that had taken her to the depths of depravity was monopolising her neuronal networks. She had been so frickin' stupid, what an idiot to let that twat control her the way he did. She flicked from angry to inquisitive...something wasn't right, he wasn't the type to give up, she knew he thought of her as his, a mere possession and he wouldn't have given her up that easily. Imagine if she ever bumped in to him, these thoughts whirred around and they excited her and after the excitement came the guilt.

That night she dreamt of drugs and alcohol, she was properly wasted. Drugged up, sexy, loose and carefree. At one point during a particularly hedonistic moment the conservative and condescending Ann made an appearance asking 'why do you do it, its not real,' she can remember answering 'because it makes me sparkle,' and then she can remember suddenly shrinking inwards feeling dirty, tarnished. She woke up full of confusion, her dream had been so vivid, so real, it felt like a warning, her senses had been alerted she knew that, but didn't understand why, or more to the point didn't want to know why.

Fully awake now, her mind went onto more pressing matters, she was to leave today and go and shack up with Pete...even sounding it out in her mind felt wrong. Taking a couple of stabilizing breaths, she banished the dread that was rising and told herself to 'pull it together,' 'life was what you made it' and 'you make your bed, you lay in it' which was a favourite of her mother. At that moment it was as if she had just sealed her fate, she had not been kind to herself, it was as if she had just abandoned the vulnerable person she had slowly been beginning to accept. She had banished her core being into the dankness of her own dungeon, knowing she could not cope any other way.

Swinging her legs off the enormous double bed with its thick coverlet for the last time she acknowledged her ability to stay strong and smiled wryly to herself feeling alive and connected to the decision she had made. What she wasn't aware of, was her tender, fragile heart hardening as she pulled out her socks and underwear, picked out the toiletries she would take and began to pack her meagre possessions.

She ran her hand over the front of a folded sweater that lay in the open suitcase, its softness surprised her and she pulled back. Her reaction startled her, she felt the dread rising again and squashed it down with a forceful thwack of the suitcase lid, clicking it shut with its old fashioned fasteners.

Caroline was standing in the drive way looking out across the Island when Bally came out alone carrying her old suitcase. The housemates goodbyes had been filled with tears everyone's apart from Ann. She knew she would not see her, it would have been too difficult for them both. Caroline patted Bally's thigh as she pulled out of the drive, giving her one last chance to look back at the house that had been her home for the last four months. She spotted Ann at one of the top windows waving slowly, she returned the gesture by holding her hand up briefly and then turned to face the road, face the direction she was going in.

They'd been driving ten minutes and neither had spoken when Caroline pulled up in a petrol station. "Ciggies?"

"Errrrr no ta, I don't smoke, you know that!" Bally looked at her wondering why she had asked.

"Whatcha mean yer don't smoke?" Caroline looked perplexed "What you don't drink, don't smoke..."

"What do you do!" Bally piped in laughing. "Alright fuck it, get me some fags or maybe those little thin cigar things. Yeah do that ta."

"Righto love, leave it to me and FYI they're called cigarillos and it's the perfect choice for a non smoker like yerself as yer don't inhale."

"BTW when did you start smoking?

"When I stopped all the other shite and realised I needed a vice that 'ad major 'ealth risks."

"Yep lung cancers defo a major health risk, you chose well."

"That's wot I f'ought!" And off she went to make the purchases.

Bally sat in the car with all sorts of crap going round her head. *Maybe she should have a little spliff or a tiny little vodka and tonic, she didn't need to get wasted. What would be the harm in that, none probably?*

She watched Caroline at the counter, her blonde hair tied in a low pony tail splayed across her left shoulder, caught on the collar of her immaculate knee-length coat. It reminded her of her own winter coat with its beautiful blue fur trimmed collar, she wondered what had happened to her coat, who had it now? Maybe Blue had given it to another girl? She remembered wearing it earlier on in the year when it was really cold in January or February, stomping round Soho with Crystal as she was known then. So much had changed, what had really happened to Blue? The thought niggled her, as Caroline walked round the front of the car bumping her out of her daydream.

"Fuck it's prop'r taters out 'ere."

"I don't plan on doing it."

"Wot ever goin' outside again?" Caroline said jokingly.

"Well not until it heats up a bit."

"Let us smoke to celebrate you not gettin' owt the car for 'nother five months!" Throwing the cigarillos at her.

They unwrapped their packets relishing the sound of the cellophane crunching, click click hiss went the lighter. Wooosh inhale and hold it….ahhhhhh exhale.

BANG! Some idiot had just whacked the boot, they turned to stare at one of the garage staff. "No smoking, this is a petrol station. If you don't understand why the clues in the word petrol, which happens to be a highly flammable liquid."

"Sorry mate, very very sorry!" They chorused puffing out plumes of smoke and chuckling as they drove off narrowly missing a signboard, that sent them both off into more fits of laughter.

Chain smoking and listening to shit pop songs that they both new all the words to was easier than talking and just a bit too quickly for Bally's liking they had reached the outskirts of a village that was to be her new home. She could see the quaint little cottages along the road and the church steeple, the trees were all bare and the ground muddy.

"The 'ouse is jus' behin' the village. You can see it up on the left, ov'r there, up on the 'ill." Caroline had been to the house once before when Pete and her were discussing Bally's future. She looked across at her passenger who looked as if she was not taking it all in. "Hun, if you don't wanna do this, we can go back to mine? Api told me she wanted you to stay wiv er as well."

"No, no I'm fine, I need to do this Caro, I just need to do it this way, it will be fine. Alright?" Her heart was beating steadily and she knew it was the perfect place to lose herself. She wouldn't be there long and was intrigued about his daughters, about him. And not forgetting she'd agreed to do it, she'd made her choice.

They drove up a curved driveway to an enormous Edwardian house. Lights shone from every room and as Caroline pulled up outside the stone flagged front porch, the door opened. He'd been waiting.

Stepping quickly to Bally's side of the car he opened the door and helped her out.

"Ello girl." The greeting was familiar and comforting and having her door opened made her feel a bit special, which made her shy.

"Hello Pete, thank you for letting me stay." He smiled at her and called over his shoulder.

"Alright, Cryst, journey all good? Get yourselves in by the fire. I'll sort the bags."

Caroline had obviously decided not to tell Pete of her name change. Bags? What was he thinking? Bally's mind was on red alert and refused to stop whirring. They went on ahead entering a vast hallway flooded with light from a stylish gold chandelier. An ornate wooden staircase wound its way up from the burgundy tiled floor which was worn and comforting, the house was special. It was real class, stylishly understated.

Caroline nudged Bally in the ribs, "Fuckin' 'ell mate this il do eh!" They didn't have the chance to start giggling before a little girl came bounding towards them.

"Ooooh are you her, are you Bally? My names Pearl I'm the nice one, Juniper's my older sister, she's a bitch. Gracie's the little one, she's four, it was her birthday last week, she's really cute."

"Yes I'm Bally and thank you very much for coming to say hello, I'm a bit nervous and I could do with a friend. Will you show me your room later?" Fuck me thought Caroline, Bally was a natural, Jesus she didn't see that coming, as the little girl and Bally walked hand in hand towards the lounge, with its blazing fireplace, chatting like old friends. She was just taking in the sumptuous living room when Pete called through the door.

"Crystal, a quick word?"

"Yeah of course." And she followed him into another beautifully created room. This was really some pad. Shit he must have made a fortune. Pete who could read her mind, brought her back to her senses.

"I can't fank you enouf for all you've done, 'ere's a little parting gift and don't forget to grab yourself a sandwich that the nannies made for alls our lunch." His aggressive tone did not go a miss as she listened respectfully. With that he pushed a fat envelope over the table towards her, she looked at it with disbelief. Fuck she was getting dismissed!"

"Ta very much Pete, I'm going to put my 'ead round the door and say goodbye to Bally and then

I'll be off then." She got up and walked towards him and they embraced without feeling. Dread prickled her from head to toe as she went to find Bally and say a very quick good bye. They hugged and handed her a phone.

"All yer contacts are on it, give us a call 'n we can go 'n drink 'erbal tea." Caroline looked into her friends eyes.

"Thanks Caro, thanks for everything." Her voice was barely a whisper as she watched her friend walk away, glad to see her leaving it was a bit awkward the three of them being there. She'd call her later and they could get date in and chat on there own.

After a chaotic lunch, what with some very excited children and sandwiches nobody liked. Pete disappeared into his study leaving Bally to spend the afternoon combing nylon pink hair and squeezing stick thin arms into miniature lycra tops, while her youthful entourage kept a beady eye on her. Their new companion would no doubt turn back into a grown up and start saying boring stupid things like 'brush your teeth' or 'do you like school,' if she escaped their imaginary world and they weren't taking any chances.

"Are you finished?" A little voice enquired behind the closed door toilet door.

"Hey what dya mean? I only just sat down! Count

Nearly Thirteen Months

to ten." Bally replied smirking to herself. She was enjoying herself with the two youngest sisters, they really were quite something.

"Is it a number one or a number two? 'Cause if it's a number two, it's gonna be more like a hundred years and twenty days!" Gracie was full of important facts.

"No it isn't dumb bum, only when you dump. Everyone else in the world can do it as you count to ten."

"Er well just to clarify, it was a number one and I'm coming out." She flushed quickly and was out the door just in time to stop little Gracie thwacking her sister round the head with Pinkie Pie. "Oooh look how she flies." She gushed at the little girls, as she swooped The My Little Pony out of a clenched fist and flew her around the girl's heads, narrowly averting World War III.

Time flew and Bally was shocked to see it was nearly five when they all found themselves in the kitchen feeling a bit hungry. Pete had winked at her as she'd hobbled in with his two children on either leg and she had looked away shyly but glanced over to see him now watching their nanny attempting to cook a roux sauce for the macaroni cheese she was making for everyone. Ali was not the best of cooks but she did try bless her and the girls adored her.

237

A slightly concerned Pete asked if she needed a hand, she didn't, so he started grimacing at Juniper who mouthed the phrase 'I'm anorexic today.' Whilst keeping a poker straight face. The constant chatter and jokes across the room were infectious, nobody took anything seriously, it was a stark contrast to Bally's rigid and dull family mealtimes at the hands of her controlling mother and under the thumb father.

Taking in the Waltonesque family scene in front of her she just couldn't believe it. This was her ex frickin' drug dealer, playing parent of the year. It made him look really sexy. He let his girls lead the conversation, which flitted from one thing to another. Juniper was slightly wary of their new guest but after the macaroni cement broke the ice (no molars this time) she too was caught up in the fun of having a house guest.

Children, doting parent, beautiful home, Bally watched in awe as the evening closed in and it was bath time. During the rounding up of small children Bally found herself being ushered to her room by the man of the house who suggested she get an early night as she must be very tired. She wasn't, but didn't want to say anything so allowed herself to be led into the room, where he squeezed her arm affectionately, held her eye contact and closed the door in such a way, if it could speak, it would have said 'and don't come out.'

Feeling slightly uncomfortable she turned to face the room and was soon distracted. It was breathtaking with its few pieces of exquisite Edwardian furniture, the sort of stuff that wouldn't look out of place in a Sothebys catalogue. Everything was period and original and worked beautifully. Her bathroom could only be described as luxurious. Cream tiles with a dark trim covered the floor, a clawed bath stood at the end of the room, soft fluffy peach towels perched on the lip all illuminated by the soft glowing light from a golden chandelier. Had he organised all this? Was Pete into period furniture. Wow...she'd tell Caroline and they could have a laugh about it later, chuckling to herself.

As she was not tired in the least, she went through all the drawers where she came across all her meagre belongings and numerous items from her old flat. It sort of shocked her a bit to think Pete had packed her stuff up, if it had been him and unpacked for her, here in this room, I mean, she wasn't a child, she could have unpacked her stuff herself. Slightly irritated she went through the drawers again, the only thing she couldn't find were her Moccasins, maybe he'd put them downstairs.

Once again she felt slightly confused by his actions, but brushed them off as a very sweet gesture and decided maybe it was a good idea to get an early night. She had packed a few books and they lay on the bedside table. Early night it was then!

Bally slept badly, she had had nightmares that upon waking she couldn't remember. All she could recall was that it felt like it was going on all night. Tired and slightly jaded she pulled the curtains back gazing out across the sweeping Kent countryside, which was covered in a blanket of snow, it was as if she had been transported to another world. Pete had told her last night that snow was coming, which had set his children into a flurry of their own excitement. He had held her stare at that point and she had looked away. Fuck what was she doing here? And with that thought, jumped back into bed and fell fast asleep.

A knock on the door woke her up. "Hey Bally if you're awake brekkie's downstairs and Pete said to say he won't be back till late."

"Oh hi Ali, morning! Ok I'm coming down." Caroline had given her a phone, which had a new number, but had all her contacts on it. She decided to charge it (good place to start) and make contact with Caroline who had left in a hurry last night, she'd been really weird, she definitely needed to talk to her and her Mum, who to be fair was always weird. Yep she was gonna have to make that call. Maybe do that one tomorrow.

Once out of bed she realised how much better she felt knowing Pete wasn't in the house. It was a bit awkward, it would take some getting used to no doubt, she spoke encouragingly to herself, even though 'doubt' wasn't so sure. She'd better get back to work and earn some money and get somewhere proper to live. Arghhhh, add phone Gareth to the list of unpleasant things to do. No fuck Gareth she could get a job somewhere else. She plugged in the phone and decided to forget about her 'to do' list until after lunch and anyway the phone needed charging.

12 DECEMBER

'Oh, gin
How could you treat me this way.'

Oh Gin, Lou Reed

The snow was back again and Bally still hadn't gone back to work. She called Gareth and fobbed him off with an ineffectual flu story. He knew it was bullshit and had told her so, now she was avoiding him and Api who were desperately trying to get her back to Chambers. Caroline had called a few times and asked if she wanted to go out. She did not!

In fact, she didn't want to do anything but hide away. She'd spent the last few weeks hiding away, running around after children and keeping herself out the way of Pete who had an amazing talent for making her feel really shite about herself. She felt inadequate in his company, always like she wasn't getting it right and doing things that he didn't like. Not that he'd say anything, of course he

Nearly Thirteen Months

wouldn't, it probably wasn't as bad as all that any way. She was no doubt being a bit oversensitive and dramatic. He'd told her a few days ago that she wasn't very good at remembering things and looked a bit confused. She had started to doubt if she had really felt funny about some of the things he said to her.

She didn't know why she felt so desperate. When Pete spent a few hours with his children she felt left out, jealous and on these occasions she chastised herself for being silly. Desperately wanting his attention, but not knowing why it was as if she wasn't living her own life and wondered whether she had ever? She had taken to having a little sip of something from the alcohol cupboard in the kitchen and didn't want anyone to know she was doing it, so took a little from each bottle, it made her feel better.

There was a pot on the counter with money in for household stuff if she needed to buy anything, there was at least £300 in it, she could buy a bottle, but then again, Pete had said light heartedly 'make sure you get a receipt and stick it in there as well, otherwise the kids get accused of stealing.' She didn't want him to know she was drinking it was her secret.

When she'd had a few too many sips and was pacing around her room when the rest of the house was asleep. She took to overthinking the conversation she'd had with her mum a few weeks ago.

"Yer like a bad penny, I don't think I need to say more, do I?"

'No...hi bally what happened to you, I've been so worried, are you ok'

"You're father has been beside himself and it's me that's gotta deal with him missy, not yerself, is it now?"

'lay on the guilt'

"Dya know what you've put us through? No I can't says yer do, as its only yerself yer think about."

'Irish brogue getting thicker and thicker, she could feel the spittle land on her face from her mother's vitriolic mouth'

"So I suppose, you'll be wanting something, some help or something to pull yer out the hole yer dug yerself? Drugs? Well I've never been so ashamed in all me life."

"Er no Mum, I was just phoning to say hello and that I was on the mend."

"Well that's very kind of yer to grace us ideeots with yer presence."

"I didn't mean it like that Mum, what I meant was..."

Nearly Thirteen Months

"Well what does it matter now Bally you've brought shame on the whole family. Drugs! I'm just so shocked you could do something like this to us. Yer father's beside himself..."

"Yes mum you said before. I am really sorry, I didn't..."

"Don't get pissy wit me girl! It's me that has to pick up the pieces here. Good bye Bally and I expect you to come for Christmas this year, so we can keep an eye on you. Well I never...drugs!"

"Bye Mu..."

The phone went dead. She slumped into a chair and tried her hardest to hold back the tears that began to pop out her tightly shut lids. Tense and angry she wondered why that conversation had gone so wrong, why hadn't her mum asked her what had happened or if she was alright?

The pain she felt was like a punch in the stomach. She was glad to be sitting as she doubted very much if she could stand at that moment. She reached into the desk draw and took out a bottle of rum that she had found in a box downstairs, she'd left the box in the cupboard so nobody would be notice it missing. Holding on to the neck for support she swigged again and again. Thank fuck for alcohol, without it she wouldn't survive.

Days went past where she struggled to get through

the day without a drink, she was quickly getting through the booze cupboard and had started replacing the clear alcohol with water, she didn't touch the single malts knowing it was Pete's tipple. Knowing she couldn't sustain the practice she began to work out a plan to get more alcohol. Which was pretty difficult if you didn't have any money and didn't want anyone to know you were doing it.

Her choices flittered between selling something, doing a trade of some sort, stealing money from Pete's office (she'd never been in there but assumed there would be a handful of petty cash lying around) and lastly, cracking open the children's piggy banks (hopefully never an option, but she was getting desperate).

She decided on selling something and going to Riverton which was the big town seven miles away to hock it in one of those 'we buy anything for cash' shops on the high street. She didn't have anything to sell so she would have to nick something from the house. Something small that nobody would miss but nothing too valuable.

Once the decision to steal had been made she started a reccy of the house. A carriage clock in the spare bedroom caught her eye. Perfect she thought, no one comes in here it won't be missed and as she swiped it off the mantelpiece she made a quick sign of the cross and thanked a god she didn't believe in, by raising her eyes upward, bringing her palms together as in prayer whilst mouthing the words 'god bless you.'

Later on that day with her booty in a shoulder bag she headed downstairs shouting "Ok Ali I'm off and I'm taking the car, like we agreed this morning. If you need anything just buzz on the mobile. I won't be long an hour or so."

"Bye Bally, just as long as you're back before the school run at three you can keep it. Bye hun!"

"Will do and don't forget I'll cook dinner!" Bally had gotten rather fond the young Australian housekeeper/nanny. Her cooking was appalling but she made up for it with her easy going nature and dry humour. With Ali safely out of the house she was free to roam the kitchen and the plan was to concoct an extremely cheesy cauliflower, with some extremely small kitchen assistants. They'd have fun and Bally could have a proper drink. Jumping into the car she could feel the sweat rise up her back, pulling off her coat and winding the window down she took off winding her way down the narrow country lanes.

She wasn't used to the country lanes and what with that, her racing heart and the fact she had her foot too hard on the accelerator she nearly skidded into a ditch as she braked too hard on a corner. Sliding out of the bend in second gear she willed herself to 'calm the fuck down' and took the rest of the journey at a more sedate pace, as her palms continued to sweat and slip all over the steering wheel.

Riverton was a town where all the locals looked like inbreds. Bally hurried along the icy pavement avoiding eye contact and the ugly glare from low quality tinsel and cheap decorations. Shit she'd have to find somewhere to hide out over Christmas, fuck another thing to deal with. Where the fuck was this place she cursed, she'd already passed a Morrison's which was to be her alcohol stop. Suddenly the bright yellow sign came into view and she was opening the door which made a tired looking Santa dangling on a string flap up and down against the dirty glass.

"Hello sir, I was wandering if you could help me?"

"I'll try love." The pawn shop manager was an enormous blob of misery. His miserable grey sunken face perched atop an equally grey morbidly obese torso. Unfortunately, all too clear as the man sat in an overstretched, red string vest. Bally shuddered inwardly at the sight of him but was not to be deterred.

"I've got a carriage clock I want to sell." She said in her best Barrister voice whilst taking the timepiece out of her bag and setting it upon the counter." Suddenly a horrible smell came from where the blob was stationed, she closed her mouth and inched back.

"Is that right now." He replied without moving his lips or looking up from his biker magazine. It wasn't a question and Bally had dealt with his type numerous times before. She kept quiet. He'll break in the end, he just didn't know it yet. Fixating on the numerous post-it-notes, there must have been about 500 of them behind his head she relaxed into the deafening silence. Reading one by one she started from the top left hand corner, anticipating a long wait.

jp silver signet

carol – 07456 235 235

34 Monrose St – Pick Up 5pm

Gabi can't make it till later, she says sorry

100, 323, 346

Each yellow note in various stages of decay, some curled and faded, others bright and fresh. One had a large coffee stain with hardly visible pencil scribbled across it. She felt herself slipping away into a tiny yellow paper micro universe.

"Ahem, hello lady." Ha ha she knew he'd be the first to break. She answered slowly as if she was doing him a favour.

Jane De Croos

"Yes"

"Its not the best I've seen but not the worse. I'll give you £30 for it."

"Its a George III, rosewood and brass by B Benjamin, circa 1820-1824. I want £100." Bally had had a quick google at home and new the price an ebay sale could get.

"Done"

They shook and he eyed her trying to work out why she was so desperate for cash. She didn't look like a junkie but it was definitely something otherwise why would you be hocking a £600 clock for £100?

With a handful of grubby £10's in her pocket she headed for the Morrisons changing their slogan to the more appropriate *'lots of alcohol costs less.'* The adrenaline flooding her body felt wonderful, she was charged with it. Looking up at the crisp blue sky and with its soft billowing clouds a feeling of intense joy washed over her.

Energised and purposeful she strode to the hard spirit section making a note of its exact aisle number, knowing she'd be here again. Ahhh perfect, a litre of 38% proof vodka only £12.99 Morrison's special offer. Just one would be enough, she didn't want to get caught clanking back into the house. Driving back she placed her hand over the bottle that was in her open bag, in full view on the front seat next to her. A slight sickness was present in her stomach, in her throat, she knew she shouldn't be doing this, but also knew that she didn't really care. Patting the bottle she pushed the bag away shutting the contents from eyesight.

Back home she breezed upstairs shouting 'I'm back'. Ali knew not to ask her anything, but she would tell Pete when he asked if she'd been out. The whole set-up was really really weird, I mean didn't Bally know that Pete was keeping tabs on her? She felt a bit mean reporting on her, but the money was so good. She carried on loading the washing machine, telling herself just a year, save the money and then back travelling...yay!!!

Whilst Ali was dreaming about her next holiday, Bally was back in her room, with the door firmly closed. She quickly tipped the clear liquid into a glass she had only that morning stolen from the dishwasher. The warm liquid burnt as she chucked it back. And then she had another and another. The buzz was glorious, fuck that felt so good. Hearing Ali go out to get the kids she roamed the house looking at things, prying open cabinets and storage cupboards. She walked past Pete's study, the vodka had given her courage, she opened the door.

Pete was in a cafe six miles away, reading the paper and having a cup of tea, when he got the ping on his phone. Looking down he saw the message from SpySecure.

    camera activated

    area: room1

Opening the App he leaned over the table to get a closer look at the screen. Then all of a sudden he could see Bally in his study. He watched her intently, he'd been wondering when she'd have a nose. She walked across to the desk and flipped through some papers on the desk and then sat in his swivel chair and twirled in it like a child. Going through the drawers and not finding anything of importance she looked quite bored until she discovered the single malt and a glass. Sniffing the glass, it was clean, he always made sure it was, she poured herself a drink, a very large drink he noted.

Gulp...that felt good she thought, then necked the entire contents. She wanted another, but knew Pete would notice, so put the bottle and glass back, giving the glass a quick wipe on her jumper. By now as she was suddenly feeling very drunk and very tired. Pete watched her get up and stagger to the door. She was drunk, drunk on one glass, that quick? No chance. She must have had a fair few before she'd got to his study. Well at least he knew what she was up to all day now. The screen went blank and a message popped up:

    camera deactivated

Pete only had a camera in his study so he put the phone down and wondered what he was going to do with her. He knew she was desperate for his affection and he'd done his best to ignore her and so when the time came she would be totally hooked. His method had never failed, but what with her drinking again made her desire for alcohol probably greater than her desire for him. And he needed her to be desperate for him, he needed her to be smitten. He'd have to keep a closer eye on her and felt that glorious stirring in his groin, so far he'd been a very patient man. He would have his prize, have her all for himself and he knew just how to do it.

His first call was to Ali. "Hello Ali and how are things with you today?" How polite he was, the young girl thought as she answered the call and at the same time not very nice. She couldn't work him out but just knew there was something untrustworthy about him. She feigned stupidity as always and started blabbing on about the kids and irrelevant stuff. "Great anyway luv." He cut in, "I need you to clear all the booze out that cupboard. I think our Juno is having a little sip on the sly. Make sure you empty all the bottles down the sink 'fore you chuck 'em. Do it today. I'll be back at 6. I 'eard Bally's cooking dinner as it's your night off? I'll text her not ta bother. Can you tell the kids I'll take 'em for dins at that pizza place. Can you 'ang on till I get back?"

"Yeah no probs mate." She sang back, wondering what was going on.

She put the phone down and went up to the primary school gates to collect Gracie and Pearl. Juniper would meet them by the car. It was all very funny, Juniper drinking? No chance, she hated even the smell of alcohol, so that only left one person. Oh dear she thought and hoped very much the whole circus wasn't going to implode before she could get the hell out of there.

Bally heard the bleep from a text on the table. A while back she had taken herself off to bed and fallen into a drunken sleep. Dry mouthed and still pissed she managed to get to her phone and take a look a the text...'*don't bother bout dinner, taking girls for pizza.*' Oh fuck she had totally forgotten about dinner, shite, but it was ok he was coming to take them out. Thank you, thank you god! And climbed back into bed taking a much needed bottle of water with her.

When Ali got home she started on the bottles and noticed no strong smell coming from the vodka bottle as she tipped it down the sink. She tasted the residue in the sink, a very watered down vodka hit her taste buds. So Bally was definitely drinking on the sly. Ali knew all about drinking on the sly as her dad had been doing it for years whilst her mum turned a blind eye. She used to find empty bottles of booze in the airing cup-

Nearly Thirteen Months

board between the towels, behind the sink in the bathroom, in the laundry basket. She never understood why her dad never just threw them out or why her mum disposed of them for him. But she knew he was a drunk and her mum was helping him stay that way. Collecting the last of the bottles and their boxes she dragged them to the wheelie bin and threw them in, smashing them as they fell.

Bally could hear the bottles breaking from her bed. As long as it wasn't her one she didn't care and fell back asleep. Then a knocking woke her. "Hey Bally, you OK? The girls were wondering how you were. I told them you weren't feeling very well. You did look a little peaky this morning?" Ali didn't know what was going on, but knew Bally could probably do with an excuse, right now.

"Oh sweetheart, thanks so much, just suddenly feel like shite. I'll be better tomorrow. Just need to rest right now."

The lie came as easy as the guilt. Laying back on the bed she heard Ali's footsteps go back down the stairs. Luckily her room was the furthest away from the other bedrooms she wouldn't have the girls running past her locked door. She felt terrible she knew they would want to see her, she had wanted to see them too. Well she had until she had gotten drunk. Curling up into a ball she lay on her bed wondering what the fuck she was doing. What the fuck was going on?

She hated herself right now, hated her lack of control. She knew she needed to stop drinking, throw the bottle out she'd just bought. And she also knew she wouldn't do it or couldn't do it. What was it the Good Doctor kept saying *'it's your choice.'* His words echoed round her head, her choice, why was it then she felt she had no choice? Scared and lonely she waited until she heard Pete come home and take the girls out before she went downstairs to make herself something to eat and found that Ali had left her a plateful of sausages and crusty bread. All that was missing was the ketchup and went to the cupboard to get it out. Her hunger rapidly abandoned her as she saw the middle shelf of the cupboard empty of all the alcohol that was previously there. The ketchup and all other condiments were as they always were on the shelf below. Only the alcohol had been taken.

Fuck. Fuck. Fuck. He was on to her. Racing back upstairs to the safety of her room she pulled out the vodka she had hidden on the shelf at the top of her wardrobe and drank heavily from the bottle. Slumping to the floor she cried, oh how much she pitied herself now. What the fuck was she going to do? She had to leave, but where to, where could she go and how would she get out? With no money, no job, she sobbed and drank, sobbed and drank. Never for a moment did it cross her mind that the booze she was gulping down might be the

Nearly Thirteen Months

problem in the first place. She was without blame, she was the victim.

She'd phone Api or Caroline she'd ask them for help, they didn't want her to stay with Pete anyway. Not Caro she couldn't hide the drinking from Caro, but Api wouldn't notice. She'd say she was just depressed had a virus or something like that and that Pete was pressure on her to get into bed. Api would love that one. The fact that he had not, made Bally shudder with shame, even Pete didn't want her. And that was the truth. Necking more vodka, she leaned out the window lighting a Cigarillo. Puff puff, sip sip ahhhh that was better. She'd be gone tomorrow and this whole thing of being at Pete's would be well behind her. Her puffy swollen face stared back at her from the windows reflection, she turned away from herself, it was better not to see.

Very late that night Pete started making calls to get Bally back into rehab for alcoholics one that worked a 12 Step Program. He knew this would be her only chance of sobriety and without that she had nothing. He would talk to her tomorrow in the afternoon, he had to be out early for a few meetings and wanted to do it before the kids got back. He'd seen this thing time and time before very rarely did an addict walk away from their addictions as easily as Bally had professed to do. She would go to rehab it was the best place for her. Whether or not she wanted to go didn't cross his mind. She was his responsibility now and he wouldn't let her down. Going to bed that night he put it all behind him and dreamt about the future and Bally being well and loving the man he was. In his dream she was very very grateful.

Bally couldn't remember any of her dreams when she woke and quite honestly didn't give a shite anyway, as she had more pressing things to deal with. Her head was literally about to explode and with her brain banging mercilessly against her skull she made a dash to the beautiful porcelain toilet and just about made it. Chucking up a watery yellowish substance she continued until the last of the green bile was up from her stomach which made her heave even more. When there was nothing left she turned her attention to her pounding headache.

She was no amateur and set to crushing two paracetamol and codeine on the side of the sink with a perfume bottle. She'd found the headache tablets in the medicine box downstairs a few weeks ago and snaffled a few strips away for a rainy day. Crush, crush, crush she worked away until the tablets were broken down, fine enough to snort. Lurching towards the door, the alcohol had really poisoned her body, she was barely able to stand up, she dug out a tenner from her bag and stumbled back into the bathroom to hoover up the whole dusty pile in two enormous sniffs as she held onto one nostril. 'Arghhhhh' her sigh was audible and animal like, as she slipped to the floor and waited for the buzz to wash over. Just as it always had.

As she lay in bed feeling very sorry for herself wondering what to do about Pete knowing about her drinking and how she was going to blag her way out of this one she heard a knock on the door and was even more startled when it opened. Hadn't she locked it last night?

"Can I come in!" It wasn't a question she noted as he was already in the door.

"Errrr not really I'm terribly unwell, virus, cold, very sick, wouldn't want you to get it and be ill and give it to the kids. Make the whole house sick. Must have picked it up when I was at the errrr library yesterday." Library? Arghhhh...shit did she just say just say library, fuck she was losing it?

"Bally I've booked you in to a clinic for alcoholics it's in Spain." Pete spoke as if he hadn't heard her. She was sick wasn't she? You'll leave now with a mate of mine he's going to give you something for the anxiety and you can have a drink on the plane." He knew a way to a girls heart!

"But, errrrrrr, I don't want to go!" Rehab, no alcohol, no, no, no! "I won't go!" That song started to go round her head... Amy someone, she couldn't remember, she couldn't think.

"Yah you will, James 'ere he's gonna give you a shot then you're gonna go." A man appeared next to him, he didn't look like a Doctor, he looked like a some Eastern European gang member. One of those on Crimewatch. She was too sick to struggle, crying big loud sobs, she felt the prick in her arm and was soon drifting off all her worries floating away.

"She'll be awake in an hour feeling vile. I'll keep her slightly medicated until we get on the plane. A promise of a drink will keep her from misbehaving. Don't worry I'll take good care of her. I'll wait for you in the car." His manner was as eloquent as his English, as he nodded just a fraction in Pete's direction to indicate his departure.

As the slightly more portly James Bond figure strode down the hall out of sight, Pete set to packing a bag for Bally that the other man had left. He went to the top draw in the desk and pulled out her passport, looking at the expiry date. All good at least she had left it where he had put it only a month ago when he had unpacked. He pulled a few items of clothing out enough for a few days so as not to raise any suspicion as customs. She could be going on a work trip. He did this with easy confidence as he was used to packing for three girls on numerous occasions.

Zipping up the bag, he threw it over his shoulder, scooped up the unconscious Bally into his arms

Nearly Thirteen Months

and headed for the driveway. He placed her gently onto the back seat throwing her shoes next to her, he tapped the roof and watched as the car pulled away slowly. Not to be the type to ponder he went back to work. The work he'd done his very best to walk away from had lured him back and now the business was growing at an alarming rate. Which meant more people, which meant more risk and Pete didn't like risk.

Alfie adjusted his mirror to look upon the back seat and see the crumpled Bally. What a shame he thought. He had two kids himself and would be horrified if they ended up like her. He hoped very much that his place he was taking her to would set her straight. In the meantime he also hoped she wouldn't give him too much trouble. City Airport wasn't far and they could have a drink together as they waited in the lounge. First Class tickets had some perks he chuckled to himself.

Bally looked a mess as Alfie dug through her bag and told her to brush her teeth, wash her face and pull a comb through her hair. On the whole he was a good natured man and was hoping he wouldn't have to show Bally his other not-so-nice side. Rattling a pill bottle brought Bally to her senses and like a dog she was doing what was requested in record time on the promise of a treat. Handing her a Diazapam she noticed it was 10mg and swallowed gratefully.

"Hello I'm Alfie, I'm going to chaperone you to Spain and get you to the clinic in Granada Province. We will fly into Granada and then take a hire car to our destination about 70km away. I want you to relax and not concern yourself with any of the details. I'm here to take care of you and all your needs. When we get in to the lounge on the other side of customs we can have ourselves a nice drink. Can you hang on until then?" His tone was beautiful, kind, warm and compassionate. This was no Albanian gangster, more like freelancing butler she felt like crying but held it together.

"Yes Alfie I can do that. And thank you very much." Her voice mimicked his in politeness. It was all she could do show her appreciation.

Bally barely noticed what was going on until they sat in the First Class lounge and the waitress came to take their order. "Double vodka and what mixer if any would you like my dear?" Alfie spoke up without hesitation.

"Fresh lime and lots of ice please."

"And I'll have a single gin and tonic with all the trimmings." Alfie very rarely drank, but wanted to gain Bally's trust hoping she wouldn't do anything stupid. "No more for me as I'm driving the other end."

The drinks came and Bally drained hers swiftly. Alfie made sure he didn't watch but caught the waitresses eye and request another for his travel companion.

Luckily, they boarded quickly with Bally only having time for another double, before take-off, before promptly falling asleep. He looked across at her face, so peaceful and at rest from her earlier agitated pre-alcohol state. She really was a very beautiful young woman and tucked a piece of hair behind her ear in a fatherly way. God bless her he thought, God bless her.

That evening with the kids in bed, Ali had been instructed to pull the sheets off Bally's bed and put away anything left out in the desk draws. Pete had already found the vodka when packing for Bally's trip and had taken it downstairs earlier. Suddenly Ali felt very sorry for the young woman who was obviously really struggling and needed help. Ali knew she hadn't just left as Pete had said because why would she have left her mobile? Looking at the phone she had found hidden inside one of the pillow cases as she stripped the bed, it started to ring and not knowing or thinking of what she was doing she answered the call from a person called Crystoline.

"Ello mate, wots the news from the manor 'ouse?" Carolines tone was full of humour.

"Ello, ello e'rth to reeeeetard! Come in fuck wit!"

"Hello" Ali replied voice trembling. "Bally's gone

and I don't know where and I'm not sure she's ok."

"'oo are ya and where are ya?" Caroline's responded swiftly, conscious that the person on the other end of the line was scared. She sounded scared. "It's alwight, you ok? Let me 'elp you."

"I don't know where she's gone!" He arranged it, she'd been drinking. I think she's an alcoholic." Ali was becoming more and more panicked. Things were not alright. She was scared. Scared for Bally and herself. "I shouldn't be talking to you."

"It's alwight, I'm Caroline, Bally's my mate. Are you the nanny? We met briefly when I dropped Bally off dya remember?" She needed to keep this girl on the line. Ali could remember the tall, statuesque blonde, who wouldn't?

"Yes I remember."

"Ok luv, wotz yer name?"

"Ali...Listen up, I don't want Pete to find out I've talked to you."

"Don't worry luv, he won't find out from me. So dya wanna tell me wot 'appened from the beginning. Is this a good time to talk, you on yer own? I'm presuming you're in the 'ouse and the kids are in bed?"

"I can talk, but will you take my number as I don't want Pete to know I've used Bally's phone. Give me five minutes and call me on my phone, I'm going to my room and I want to delete your call on this phone."

"Alright luv, good idea, I'll buzz ya in five." The phone went dead and Caroline had five minutes to wonder what the fuck had gone on? Had she gone back to Hotel Recovery?

"Hi, I can talk, but haven't got long. This guy came to pick up Bally and that was it, she's gone and I don't know where she's gone." Ali had calmed down a bit, her rational side was making some ground...maybe it was none of her business, she shouldn't get involved.

"Can you find out?" Caroline questioned, interrupting the young girls thoughts.

"Not really, unless he tells me and he won't."

"Alwight, I'll jus 'ave to ask meself. Jus ang in there and I'll buzz you back when I know more." Click the line went dead. Ali put her phone on the bed and prayed that Bally was ok, that this whole thing would just be ok.

Caroline waited an hour and called Bally's phone several times and then waited some more until she called Pete's phone. "Hello Crytsal love, hope your keeping well and how may I be of assistance?"

"Hi Pete, I'm well ta, as I 'ope you are. And yes there

is a little somefink you can do for me. I've been tryin to talk to Bally n she's not answering, she alwight?

"As well as can be expected bein' an alcoholic an all, she won't be answering 'er phone for a good while yet love. She's gone to rehab for 6 months, non communicado style. I'll let you know when she surfaces. Ta ta for now." And with that he hung up. Caroline was left speechless Pete had just dismissed her again.

She called Ali giving her the update. Caroline suddenly felt horribly alone, there was nothing she could do apart from hope that Bally would be all the better for her stint in rehab.

THE BITTER END - PART I

Granada Airport, Spain

It was gloriously sunny and warm as the unusual pair touched down in Granada and crossed the tarmac. Bally seemed slightly out of it and Alfie held her tight. They were through customs with Alfie making all the right gestures and sounds of accommodating male with drunk female to the other passengers and passport control. Jose a middle aged chain smoker, who was quite happy to grunt instead of speak was there to greet them and take them to their hire car.

"Right" said Alfie. "We've got about an hour's drive ahead of us, we're heading north." Bally suddenly slowed, I had better go to the toilet then." She was slurring her words just a bit and bumping into Alfie as they walked.

"Ok, there's a loo just up there by the exit." Alfie said, holding her up. "You gonna be ok in there on your own? If you want I can come in with you?" His voice was full of concern, Bally felt a twinge of guilt.

"Give me a few minutes eh cause...I need to properly go if you know what I mean..couldn't do it on the plane." She mumbled bumping into him.

"Yes of course..say no more." Ahhh he thought that was why she went to the toilet for so long. He was clocking her every move and was satisfied with her explanation. The doors to the toilet banged open and swished closed as he saw her stumble in.

Pressing her back against the door she immediately started scanning the toilets for an escape route. Bingo there was a small window next to the last cubicle. Dragging the dustbin to the wall Bally was suddenly very alert as she hauled herself onto the dustbin straddling it either side and pushing against the window that opened easily.

Thank god she had stuck her fingers down her throat to make herself sick on the plane. Vomit up all the alcohol she had drunk earlier knowing she would need to have her wits about her to escape. She knew when she was in England that she would probably have only one chance and this was it and not thinking of what was on the other side she pushed her tiny frame through the window going head first onto the ground with only a rusty old drain pipe to break her fall as she clutched it desperately and almost summersaulted over.

"Fuck, fuck shite." She whispered as she hit the tarmac. Looking around, crouching down she knew her only chance to get away was in a car. Heading for the car park she had to cross the airport doors where she saw Jose outside smoking. He didn't look up and she dropped her pace mingling with a few other passengers until she swerved off heading for the car park exit gate.

Her nerves were on red alert, any minute she thought she'd hear Alfie running up behind her. He'd grab her, stop her, but as she walked the only thing audible was her heart thumping. With her mind racing she couldn't believe what was happening, only this morning she had been in Pete's house, under his scrutiny and now she had escaped him. She knew she wasn't in the clear yet, as she scanned the car park, requesting the God she didn't believe in to help her out, once again.

Moments later two young men in a battered yellow Fiat Punto whistled to her and for the first time in her life she responded. Swaying her hips slightly she smiled, flicking her head back. "Hi there, do you speak English?" The driver pulled over abruptly. "For you Señorita I will do anything." He cooed in his perfect English over the well muscled tanned chest of his passenger. Bingo, thought Bally.

"I need your help, my boyfriend and I have just had an argument and he's left me here. I need a lift into Granada." She teased, doing a little sad face.

"My darling, everything and anything for you, come with us we look after you. You be ok now!" Falling back onto the seat she stayed low and they introduced themselves as Jose (the driver) and Mateo, they were cousins. They were very sad also as they had just dropped of another cousin who was going back to work in Germany. They could all be sad together Mateo suggested, good idea thought Bally lets go drown our sorrows.

As the ticket barrier went up and the little Fiat shot out, Alfie was pushing open the door of the last toilet and glancing up at the open window. "Fuck it." He cursed under his breath. She was gone. Running outside to find Jose who was waiting outside smoking he shouted. "Car, now, start running, I've lost the girl." Jose who was not to be hurried informed the rather harassed man that he was not to worry.

"What are you talking about? Just get me the car!" Alfie who by nature was a gentle man was going to start to getting angry.

"Es good, she señorita, she in car, yellow car." He motioned flicking ash and sauntering towards the parking lot.

"What you saw her?" Alfie was fronting up to this man, who seemed oblivious to the severity of someone running away.

"Si si Señor." He said causally walking towards the

Nearly Thirteen Months

hire car. Handing over the keys and some paperwork to sign, Jose lit another cigarette and sauntered off

"Shit...how the fuck did this happen." Alfie cursed under his breath, gunning the Toyota out of the lot.

Jose seemed to be in a terrific rush as they sped round tight bends hurtling towards the city centre. He knew a great bar tucked away from the tourist trail, they both assured her she'd love, Bally didn't disagree. Parking rather erratically they located the bar which was small and stained dark brown and full of men smoking and laughing. They found a table then they got drunk, all three of them or that's what two of them thought. Bally took regular trips to the toilet and stuck her fingers down her throat relieving her blood steam of the potential alcohol intake. She was acting drunk, flirting and watching Mateo with his wallet casually placed in his open jacket pocket slung over his chair. She'd soon have her chance as she laughed gaily at their pathetic masculine prowess.

In the meantime, Alfie was in the city centre some ten minutes after Bally and her new companions were already in the bar. He made the call to the furiously bad tempered Pete. "Find her." Pete was not a man to mix his words and Alfie was uncomfortably aware of the consequences. Parking the car he started making his inquiries. Where do alcoholics go? She'd be with a man and they'd be down a back street, she couldn't stay hidden forever.

Bally had her chance, she bumped into Mateo's chair falling to one knee. She slipped her hand into his coat pocket, pulled out his wallet and tucked it down her t-shirt. With the help of her very tipsy new friends she was back on her feet and heading for the front door stating she needed to make a call and would be five minutes. Waving coquettishly as she weaved her way through the tables she was out in seconds and was heading for the bus terminal which she'd clocked on the way in.

"Malaga por favor."

"Si señora, de una sola mano?"

"Errrrr…"

"You go no come back?"

"Yes just to Malaga."

"Si, de una sola mano, 10 euros señora"

"Gracias, thank you." Luckily for her Mateo had a wallet full of Euros. The gods once again were shining upon her.

"Bus, go this one," as the ticket office girl pointed her in the right direction.

Ticket in hand she was on it like a shot. It was a two hour trek to Malaga so she might as well get some sleep and got comfy as the bus pulled out. Meanwhile, a rather pissed off Jose and Mateo after realising they had been done, were back in their beat up yellow Punto shouting at each other. Which is what Alfie witnessed as they pulled up at a junction. Yep he thought to himself she'd definitely done those two over. Ok where to now, where would she go now he mused? She'd get the hell out of here, that's what she'd do. He needed a taxi rank and fast. Unfortunately, Alfie's Spanish wasn't great and nobody had seen a woman going anywhere in a hurry. Getting back into his hire car the only thing left was to take a chance and head to Malaga. It was big enough for her to get lost in and if it was him on the run that's where he'd go.

Bally by now was formulating another plan. She needed to call Caroline and get some back up. As soon as she pitched in Malaga she'd make the call and get her old chum to sort her out a hotel and wire her some dollar. And then she could sit tight and wait to be rescued. And possibly have a little drink. The bus pulled into the terminal as she woke up and to say she was feeling pretty shite, would have been polite. Tired, with a mouth like a carpet she hauled herself off the bus into the bright sunshine. Ok go get some change and look for a call box. She bought some water and downed it all and went to make the call to Caro's HQ thank god she had a work address and phone number the call collected immediately. "Bally is that you, what the fucks goin' on mate." The call ID had flashed up a foreign dial code.

"Caro, I'm in trouble I need you to wire me some money I don't have my passport, nothing!"

"Fuck what 'appened fuck this is not good, where are you?"

"Malaga, find me a hotel and book in and sort it for me, I'm near the bus terminal."

"Awight done, I'll buzz you back on this number stay by the phone...you alwight?"

"Yeah I'm alright, I'm alright, talk in a bit."

Caroline was on her laptop searching for airbnb's she knew she would have trouble checking her into a hotel without her passport. But online she could use her own details. Perfect two bedroom about ten minutes from where she was La Princesa, keys in security box. Now to sort her out some money that was gonna be a bit more difficult. She made the call.

"Hi Jonnie, long time no speak. I need a favour, rather urgent one."

"Hello Crystal, how lovely to hear from you, of course I'd love to help, what can I do for you."

"I need you to drop a good friend of mine some money they're in Malaga. I need you to do it ASAP."

"I'm sure I can arrange that for you. How much and

what's the address?" Caroline secure in the knowledge that her request would be fulfilled, dropped the call. Right now to call Bally back. The foreign dialing tone rang once.

"Caro,? Caro?" Her voice came across thin and weak over the line that gently buzzed. She'd been waiting by the phone in a major state of anxiety.
"Yeah it's me. 'ow u 'oldin up?"
"I'll be a lot better when I'm off the street, with some dollar in my pocket?"

"Right remember this address Calle Heroes de Sostoa 45, there's a key box by the bins number 4545 and the flat is number 4. Say it back to me."
"45 Calle Heroes de Sostoa, flat 4, key code 4545. Can I go there now?"
"Yes mate, and you'll 'ave a visitor aft'r 8pm tonight bringin' dollar and a phone. Call me latr. Bally you're gonna be al'wight." Caroline was willing her friend to stay strong, she hadn't had the chance to wonder what the fuck had gone on, but no doubt she'd hear all about it later. "Bally, keep it together, don't you go doin' nuffin stupid now?" They both knew what she meant.

"Thank you Caroline. I'll call you later and tell you everything. God, thank you so much. Love you." Bally's voice crackled with emotion as she hurriedly put the phone down and went to find someone who could direct her to *'Calle whatever the fucky was.'*

Caroline fingered her phone nervously, somewhere along the line she was gonna have to deal with Pete. Hmmmm not something she was looking forward to, but in the meantime there was nothing else to do but get back to work. She was half-way through a new presentation about streamlining the most productive working day for the successful business woman, which she'd be delivering to an auditorium of desperate females. What she really wanted to say to them was:

- None of this matters
- You'll spend a life time trying to be successful and fail
- In wanting to find a bloke you'll lose you're true self
- You'll waste decades investing in a job you hate

Haha she mused she could take a leaf out of her own book and carried on with the drivel she had previously been drafting.

THE BITTER END - PART II

Bally let herself into the clean, well-appointed apartment and made a beeline for the kitchen pulling out a glass from the first overhead cabinet she opened. Glug, glug, glug, the vodka slopped in. Thankfully, there had been a little convenience store just below her. Pulling open the balcony door, she gulped the fiery syrup and hung back a little in the shade. No need to make herself visible and went back to pour herself another and go have a nose around.

A horribly loud buzzing sound made her fall off the sofa. Blimey she must have fallen asleep. Shite who was that, Oh yeah it was probably her money drop. It was dark outside and cold in the apartment. She fumbled to the hallway and pressing all the buttons on the intercom let the stranger in. Bally stood behind the door and waited. Click, click went a pair of heels up the 2 flights. Tap, tap on the door. "Hello, I've got a parcel." The voice was English and home counties. Well that was unexpected thought Bally opening the door very slightly and keeping herself out the brightness of the corridor light. "I've put a sim card in there and my numbers on the phone if you need anything else. I'm Claire." Pushing the parcel through the door into Bally's hand she spun round and was off.

Back at the kitchen counter Bally counted the money wow €2000 that's cool, well done Caro she thought, pocketing a few hundred and stashing the rest. She needed some new clothes, but first things first she needed to eat. Knocking back another drink she was out the door heading down the back streets towards a pizzeria she'd walked past earlier. She was fully aware Alfie would be on her trail and went to the back of the restaurant where she ate like a horse, much to the delight of the owner, who laughed and joked with her in broken English about her tiny frame.

Full up and feeling good she made her way back to the apartment. Crossing a little plaza she wound up a different back street which she was sure would take her to the junction she needed. A dodgy looking couple were fiddling about with a small wrap in an old doorway of a derelict building. She clocked them immediately and they glanced at her suspiciously. Without quite knowing what she was doing she had her hand in her pocket and was standing a few paces in front of them.

"Sorry I don't speak Spanish, I'm sick I need what you've got and I'll pay you this." She held a handlful of Euros out in front of her and then held it to her chest. The woman shouted something at the man who suddenly grabbed Bally and pushed her into the doorway, snatching the money out of her hand. Bally's heart raced. Shit fuck, she was gonna get mugged and probably beaten up. She put her hand out for the wraps, always the optimist.

"Ok you doon't worry, I 'elp you. Thees veery good." The woman said in her heavily accented English placing two large wraps into Bally's hand, as the man pushed her out of the doorway. Both characters had missing teeth, his skin hung from haggard cheek bones and her bottom lip drooped, making her her look slightly deranged. They were definitely not the sort of people you'd be drawn too, unless of course you needed what they needed.

Bally didn't hang around. Her whole body was trembling, shite she'd done it! Her heart was thumping so loudly she could feel it banging against her rib cage. Jogging down the street, she was sweating. She needed some supplies and was glad she'd put the change from the restaurant in another pocket. She needed foil and a lighter. They were definitely heroin users. Thank you God! Yes life was good and the dear Lord had once again provided.

Back in the safety of the apartment, she got ready. Reliving the last ten minutes in her head, a crazy smile plastered across her face. How had that just happened, one minute walking home, then next scoring in a city she'd just arrived in and was in hiding. Fuckin' great she was in for a fuckin' great night now. She'd call Cryst, errrr Caro in the morning! She didn't care about anything or anyone anymore, the addict had surfaced and was in control. Bally was beyond helpless and had no problem succumbing. She knew what she was doing and she didn't care. There was only one thing to do and that was to get high and she couldn't wait.

In the dim lighting on the plush grey sofa she ran her first line for the first time in five months, the rush was sensational. It washed over her fragile body and mind, wrapping her up, saving her from her true self. She was truly grateful, as a single tear slid down her face. Glug, glug went the vodka from the bottle. Hiss, hiss went the lighter on the foil. Time passed...as she lapsed in and out of consciousness, her mind whirred and slowed. And she kept taking hit after hit. Finally, around 3am she passed out, the glass she'd been holding onto, rolled off the sofa and smashed against the cold tiled floor, the bent foil in her left hand rested in her palm.

Around 4am she started to choke on her own vomit, with her head back and without the luxury of a gag reflex, which would, if you weren't completely off your head, kick in and wake you up. She started to choke, spluttering as the heavy doughy pizza lodged in her throat. And she kept on choking and spluttering as lumps of half digested dough, tomato and cheese flew out her mouth and dribbled down her chin. She still didn't wake up and within two minutes she was dead from asphyxiation.*

Caroline had gone to bed that night praying for the safety of her friend. She'd booked a flight and would be in Malaga by the morning. She'd also called her new friend, the wolfish man that had got to know Bally they spoke for a long time. She was comforted by his voice, comforted by his masculinity. They agreed to meet up when she came back. She told him "I need you."

"As I need you." Was his swift reply as he hung up.

Her Malaga contact had been in touch and said the delivery had been made. Caroline went to bed that night after trying to get through to Bally and getting no answer, she assumed she was already tucked up in her bed and decided to get an early night herself. By 8am the next morning she was walking out of Malaga airport and was first in the taxi queue. Result she thought as she was eager to see her friend, eager for a catch up and gossip about Pete. Bally had escaped, what the fuck was all that about? The taxi pulled up outside a swish apartment block.

'Briiing' the doorbell went. Caroline tried it again and then checked that she had the right door number. 'Briiiiiiing' still nothing. Then she tried her phone. Nothing. Getting a little bit anxious, a tiny gnawing feeling crept up and rose in her throat, she could taste bile. Hmmmm plan B and went to find the key lock-box where she found the 2nd set of keys and let herself in. Click clack went her sandals on the white tiles as she went up the two flights of stairs rather apprehensively, she did not have a good feeling about this. At the door the key turned easily, too easily, as she gingerly pushed the door open and called her name, the familiar smell of burnt heroin came to greet her along with the acrid stench of vomit. No no no..her heart quivered as she forced herself to carry on into the room. The blinds were closed and a lamp on the coffee table produced a dim yellowy light upon the figure slouched on the sofa.

Ballys head was back but she was not moving, Caroline wondered whether briefly if she was asleep but was now preparing herself for the worse. Coming forward she walked round the table to face her friend and took in the scene unfolding in front of her. The vomit covered t-shirt, the smashed glass on the tiles, foil still loosely placed in an open palm, a lighter on her lap, the light brown powder on the table. A deep, deep sadness engulfed the room, sucking all the life from it as Caroline literally gasped for air, trying desperately to understand what was going on in front of her, what she could see as plain as day.

Ballys open gaping mouth was covered in dried sick, her eyes were shut and her skin an unnatural grey pallor. Going to her she placed two fingers on an upturned wrist. Nothing. Her skin was cold. She was dead, her friend was dead. Caroline sat next to her and held her lifeless hand and said goodbye squeezing it hard. She didn't cry, it was too late for that.

Caroline would call the police and she would call Pete and Pete would call Alfie. Bally was dead. It was over.

*The majority of deaths from drug poisoning or misuse in 2017 involved accidental poisoning, rather than mental and behavioral disorders, suicide (intentional poisoning or death from undetermined intent) or assault. In England and Wales, 74% of all drug poisonings (79% for males and 65% for females) and 80% of drug misuse deaths (83% for males and 72% for females) were attributed to this category. (Deaths related to drug poisoning in England and Wales: 2017 registrations, Office of National Statistics.)

ABOUT THE AUTHOR

I wrote this for myself. It's my first novel and I wrote it without a plan or a draft and never did any rewrites. Its taken 4 years. I started when I fell pregnant with my second child which was hard going as carrying children doesn't suit my personality. Then when my son was 1 and my daughter was 7 we fled a domestic abuse situation, luckily securing a place in a high risk category women's refuge. That was seriously stressful, my head was all over the place. I can remember thinking OMG I'm a complete mess. But things change as they always do and I've left that person behind. This book is for the woman I've become, the one I'm just starting to get to know.

Thank you for taking the time to read this work and I very much hope you know that I am truly grateful.

All my love

Jane De Croos

Jane xx

Printed in Great Britain
by Amazon